The Seven Rings of Man's Destiny
Book II:
Jimmy and the Silver Ring of
Prophecy

The Seven Rings of Man's Destiny Book II:

Jimmy and the Silver Ring of Prophecy

ISBN: 9780998426037

Contents

To my children,

for their patience

Chapter One:

The New Ring Bearer

It was dawn when the four of them arrived in Asia, still unaware of their exact location. Before deciding to take another step, Ori and the boys surveyed the new terrain. Ori looked behind them at the two pillars from whence they had teleported. He could tell by the calligraphy that they were somewhere in China.

As they moved forward, they noticed a small, Chinese dwelling next to an icy body of water. They observed the reddish, curved roof and the red pillars in front and the seemingly paper-thin, manila walls.

Ori paused in front of the abode to concentrate.

"I sense a Guardian," he said, looking side to side at the home, hoping someone friendly would come forth to welcome them.

"Should we knock?" asked Ryan, looking at Ori and then to Jimmy and Parelo, who stood by, taking in the scenery. Ori turned to Ryan, smiled, and then began walking up the stone steps to the door.

1

Knock! Knock! Ori rapped twice on the white, wooden door. After a few minutes had passed, the door opened.

"May I help you?" asked a middle-aged Chinese woman. She glanced at them suspiciously with her small, dark eyes. She had shiny black hair pinned up in a bun with a few gray streaks and was wearing a silver and white martial arts uniform. She didn't look old to them; she looked fit and ready for the unknown.

Ori bowing, "My name is Ori. I am the Guardian of the Azure Ring of Water. These are my friends. We are searching for the Ring Bearer of Prophecy," he paused, "We believe he may be in danger."

The woman looked at Ori and then again at the boys, carefully observing and deliberating, weighing the message she had just received. She knew that she couldn't afford to trust the wrong people.

"Come in friends," she stated finally, "You are all expected." Ori removed his sandals, and the boys, observing, silently followed suit. Once inside, Ori bowed and then the boys bowed to the woman in silver.

The woman, bowing to them, spoke again:

"Follow me, please. Lu Ya is waiting for you." Ori and the boys followed the woman into another room. Once there, the woman moved quietly towards a figure sitting with his legs crossed and facing the opposite way.

"Lu Ya," she said, bowing, "your friends have arrived." The boys could tell right away that Lu Ya had been meditating.

Lu Ya stopped meditating, rose slowly to his feet, and bowed to the woman.

"Thank you, Wei Lin," he said, and then he turned and came towards us.

As soon as he had come within a few feet of them, he smiled and bowed. Taking their cues from Ori, the boys also bowed.

"Welcome, friends," he beamed, "I have been expecting you." The boys noticed that he was wearing attire that was similar to Wei Lin. They also observed that he was young, but he was older than they were. They could tell that he was an adult, not a teenager.

He had short, black hair, with black eyes that were focused and missed nothing. He was shorter than Ori and the boys, smaller, too, but he possessed poise.

"Hi, friend," Ori responded. "I am Ori, the Guardian of the Azure Ring of Water. These are friends: Jimmy, Ryan, and Parelo." The young man smiled at each of them, taking them in, one by one.

Wei Lin came into the room from another. This time, like Ori and Pazou, she had a staff and cane strapped to her side.

"This is Wei Lin," Lu Ya said, introducing her. "She is my Guardian, and I am the Ring Bearer of the Silver Ring of Prophecy." As he identified himself, he placed his left arm straight out in front of his body, so all of them could marvel at the majesty of the Silver Ring.

"Wow, that's an awesome ring," Ryan said, grinning at the man. The man put his arm down and smiled at Ryan.

"Thank you, young Guardian," replied Lu Ya. "Are you all hungry?"

"Starved," Ryan said, rubbing his hand over his stomach. The boys grinned at each other and Ori, blushing a little, and nodding to Lu Ya.

After consuming several small bowls of noodles and rice, Lu Ya took them outside. They followed a trail that led behind their home. Ori and Lu Ya walked ahead, while the boys stayed behind, looking at the scenery.

Jimmy observed that Wei Lin was cautiously flanking them. For some reason, he felt compelled to speak with her.

"Hi, Wei Lin. I'm Jimmy," he said. Wei Lin looked over at him for a moment and then she faced forward. She didn't speak for a second, as he walked alongside her. Jimmy could feel himself beginning to sweat nervously. He didn't know how to react to her silence.

Finally, she spoke to him:

"I know who you are, young man. I also know what you represent..." She became quiet, allowing Jimmy to absorb her words. "As a Guardian, it is my duty to study the power of the *Seven* and the history of our ancestors." She continued walking in silence.

She must mean the seven rings, Jimmy thought to himself.

Ryan and Parelo walked quickly to catch up with them.

"Is it true that all Chinese people know Kung Fu?" Ryan asked, curiously. Wei Lin smiled slightly but didn't lose sight of Lu Ya and Ori.

"No," she replied and continued to walk. Ryan, not knowing how to react to her terse reply, decided to keep silent.

Ori and Lu Ya paused in front of them. They turned to face each other. Wei Lin stopped, observing their every movement, and the boys paused, as well, wondering why Ori and Lu Ya had stopped so abruptly. They couldn't make out what they were saying, but they could tell from Ori's facial expressions that their conversation had taken a serious turn.

"Gorlev *will* find us," Ori said, his brows attempting to merge.

"Yes, very soon," Lu Ya replied, smiling confidently. "We all must be ready."

Ori sighed, nervously, nodding his head.

"What is the extent of your foresight?" he inquired, trying to interpret Lu Ya's unexpectedly optimistic answer.

"I can see glimpses of my future and the future of those around me. But, I cannot see my end or the end of this war," he explained. "What I do know is that our friend, Jimmy, will decide it. For the time being, this is what I see. I will keep trying."

Ori raised his head and his eyes widened at this revelation. He turned to gaze at Jimmy for a few moments, as did Lu Ya, smiling in his direction. Jimmy noticed and swallowed hard, looking back and forth at them, wondering what Lu Ya had said. Wei Lin cut a sharp glance at Jimmy, and then she looked back in front of her. Ryan and Parelo studied each one of their faces.

"Well, looks like we're safe," Ryan said, trying to lighten the mood and placing his right hand on Jimmy's left shoulder.

That night, as everyone slept, Jimmy worried about the secret conversation that had taken place between Ori and Lu Ya. He decided to go outside for some fresh air. As he sat on the steps in front of the home, he thought about Zoonee. He wondered how she was doing and when he would see her again.

He heard the door to the home slide open behind him. He turned quickly; and, to his surprise, it wasn't Ryan. It was Wei Lin. She slowly sat down beside him to his right and laid her staff down to her left.

"Can't sleep?" she asked, turning to make eye contact with Jimmy.

"No, Ma'am," Jimmy answered, still peering into her dark, mystical-like eyes.

"Good. Good to be worried. It means you care about *who you are* and *what you must do*. Not everyone worries," she explained.

"But, what if I can't do what I *must*? What if it's too hard?" Jimmy asked.

"Confucius say effort means love. Who can defeat *love*?" she asked, rhetorically. With that, she got up and began to go inside. As she slid back the door, she turned back to him.

"Get some sleep. You will need it for your training," she smiled.

The next day Wei Lin led the boys to a small meadow to practice. Ori and Lu Ya followed, too, eager to watch the lessons.

"What kind of training is this?" Ori asked, looking on and standing by Lu Ya.

"She will teach them to combine their powers with Kung Fu, just as she taught me when I was a boy. Their powers will be more streamlined and concentrated."

Wei Lin helped the boys form a triangle, and then she began.

"This is Tiger Claw," she said, as she curved her fingers sharply. Then she put on a dazzling display of the martial art's style. The boys marveled at her fluid, forceful bodily movements.

"Now, you try," she commanded. "Stop the arm. Hit the nose. Circle. Grab the face. Grab the groin," she modeled for them. The boys looked at each other and grinned. Then they began practicing what she had shown them.

"Only time for one style. Will help you to focus your gift," she explained to them. She stopped in front of Jimmy, as he was practicing the form. "You can't always use power. Must know how to defend one's self."

She moved to her left and down to face Parelo, as he repeated her movements.

"Must control self. Bring forth the tiger as you perform," she instructed. Then she moved back to her right and down to face Ryan. "Will use staff to mimic the tiger. Become more powerful." She moved up and back in front of Jimmy. "Use power to form the Tiger Claw."

That night, the boys were sore and fast asleep, all but Jimmy, who couldn't sleep. He kept wondering about the conversation that had taken place between Ori and Lu Ya and why Ori had not chosen to speak with him about it. *It wasn't like Ori to keep secrets from him*, or at least that's what he thought.

Again, he heard the door to the house slide open, and Wei Lin walked out. Jimmy realized that Wei Lin was a Guardian, too, so she was always on guard, night and day. This time, she didn't sit beside him.

"Come," she motioned to him, as she walked down the stone steps. Jimmy didn't question; he just followed Wei Lin to the frosty meadow. "Do Tiger Claw," she requested. Jimmy did as he was told, along with the other movements she had taught them.

"Now, do Tiger Claw with power," she instructed. Jimmy's eyes and mouth began to glow as he performed portions of the style. Without warning, Wei Lin threw a stone at him. Jimmy stopped.

"Ow!" he exclaimed, as the stone hit him in the chest. "Why did ya do that?" he asked, perplexed.

"Do Tiger Claw. Block stones," she said.

"Okay," Jimmy replied, starting over again.

Wei Lin hurled a smooth stone at his head. Jimmy's eyes grew large, but he continued to perform the style and deflected the stone. Jimmy paused for a moment, amazed by what he had done.

"How did that happen? I blocked the stone," he said, smiling at Wei Lin.

"Yes, you did. Why surprised? Your power comes from Poseidon, Jimmy," she explained. "How you not know this?"

"Well, I..."

"Well, now you know. Block stones."

Jimmy started over again but, this time, Wei Lin threw three stones, which Jimmy successfully diverted all around him while practicing the ancient art.

After they had finished, they headed back to the house. On the way, Jimmy had questions for Wei Lin.

"So, whatever happened to Zeus' third brother, Hades? Why doesn't he have a ring?"

"Who say he doesn't?" Jimmy looked over at her for a moment. For the first time, she smiled at him. "There is a lot we not know, Jimmy. In time, the gods show those who are worthy."

"I wonder what kind of ring it would be," he said.

"Why does it have to be a ring?" she said, winking at him, as though she knew something.

The next morning, Ori woke Jimmy and asked him to walk with him up the trail. As they walked, Jimmy could tell that this invitation wasn't recreational in nature. Ori's eyes displayed concern.

"I need to confide in you, Jimmy. But you cannot tell the others...not yet," he said, seriously. Jimmy nodded and prepared himself.

"A long time ago, there was a German boy who had become a Ring Bearer. He was a prodigy, and he exhibited great promise. He befriended a Greek boy, who was to

12

become a Guardian one day. Each day, they trained and they grew together. Until, one day, the boy's Guardian was found dead in his hut. The boy's name was Gorlev, and he had killed his Guardian," he paused, and Jimmy lifted his eyes and knew what was coming next, but couldn't believe it. "The other boy's Guardian tried to stop him. But, he, too, was killed, eaten by hot flames. The Greek boy was...me, Jimmy. And, the Guardian was...my *father*." He paused again, looking downward, but at nothing. "I have been running from him, Jimmy. I am *coward*. But, I can no longer run. He *must* be stopped, but I can't do it without you. *You* are the key, Jimmy."

Jimmy thought for a moment, and then he responded.

"I'm with you, Ori. We *will* get him, for you and for your father." Ori placed his hands on Jimmy's shoulders and looked into his eyes.

"Thank you, Jimmy," he said.

"No problem," Jimmy replied.

On their way back, Ori asked how his training was going.

"Good, different, but good," Jimmy said, grinning.

"Good. Keep listening to Wei Lin, Jimmy. She has been around for a while, and she is very wise."

"Man, I just thought I was done with training, ya know?"

"One is never done training, Jimmy," he said, placing his left hand on his right shoulder before moving ahead of him.

"Jimmy, come, we train!" shouted Wei Lin. Jimmy sighed and headed toward the meadow, trying to catch up with Ryan and Parelo.

"Hey, dude, is everything good?" Ryan asked, cheerfully. Jimmy forced a smile.

"Yeah, it's good," he lied, and then they began their training for the day.

"Now, I want you to use power with form," Wei Lin instructed. "Ryan, use staff with form." Ryan picked up his staff and began to move it and twirl it according to the style they had been practicing. He observed how it made his strikes more smooth and forceful.

"Cool, Tiger staff," he replied as he finished his demonstration.

"Parelo, your turn," Wei Lin said. Parelo's eyes began to glow green as he demonstrated to the Tiger Claw. From the bushes behind him, a China Tiger emerged and ran up to sit beside him. The others gasped in awe at this spectacle.

When he had finished, he petted the orange, white and black striped tiger, and then the animal disappeared into the yellow-tinted foliage behind them.

"That...was...awesome!" Ryan said, excited. "I'm glad you are with us." Parelo grinned and gave Ryan a high five, before turning to bow to Wei Lin. She looked over to Jimmy and nodded, indicating that he was up next.

Jimmy's eyes and mouth began to glow. Water appeared as he simulated the form, as if he were fighting a foe. The water followed his movements. Wei Lin, as she had done before, picked up a smooth stone and launched it at Jimmy's head. Jimmy, using the Tiger style, deflected the stone with water, as it formed the claw of a Chinese Tiger.

That night, they all gathered around a fire, and Wei Lin told them about the history of Chengde and the Great Garden. She shared Chinese stories and legends with them, and the boys were mesmerized by her wisdom and knowledge of her country.

During one of her tales, she explained the connections of the Greek gods to her country and people.

"Many centuries ago, Zeus and Jade met and created a covenant. The covenant stated that, if the one died or became too weak to rule, the other would become supreme."

"What happened to Jade?" Jimmy asked.

"The same thing that happened to all other gods: They became weak because people stopped believing. Zeus created the *Seven* as reminder, and Jade, with other Chinese gods, left manuscripts full of enlightenment and power. Now only kids believe legends," she said, peering down into the fire, ending her tales for the night.

"Why?" Parelo asked.

"Some say because gods ornery. Others say world better without them. They say life easier without them," she answered, reflectively.

"Is that why we are combining our powers with Kung Fu, because of the covenant?" Jimmy asked. Wei Lin, looked up and smiled at him.

"Very good, Jimmy," she spoke softly.

"Do you know any Kung Fu fighters, by any chance?" Ryan asked. The others, along with Wei Lin, laughed at his question.

A few nights later, Jimmy couldn't sleep. He was thinking about Zoonee and his family. He got up out of bed again, but this time he could hear voices, speaking Mandarin. He paused at the front door and began to listen to the conversation.

"什么时候来," Wei Lin asked.

"不久," Lu Ya replied. "Our friend is listening. Come out, Jimmy."

Jimmy slowly and quietly slid the manila door back, and stepped outside.

"Hi, Jimmy," Lu Ya greeted. "How can we help you, tonight?"

"I can't sleep. I keep thinking about my family and my girlfriend," he admitted.

"I understand. Come, let me help you," he said, gesturing for Jimmy to follow him.

Lu Ya led Jimmy down to where the fire had been burning bright several hours before, and he motioned for Jimmy to face him, the fire pit in betwixt them, the smoke still rising into the air.

"Place your hands up, palms out," he instructed. Jimmy did as he was told. "Close your eyes, and take a few deep breaths." Moments later, Lu Ya opened his eyes, and they were glowing a rich, gray hue. "Now, open your eyes, Jimmy." When Jimmy opened his eyes, he could see that Lu Ya's eyes and hands were glowing, and the smoke from the fire transformed into bright, gray flames. "Hold very still, Jimmy." Lu Ya took a deep breath and then began his prophesy.

"Your family will not be harmed by fire, but you must complete your journey to free Zoonee and your friends. You must have courage. If you fail, our world will be enslaved and many friends will be lost. This is what I see," he said, ending his prophesy. "Thanks be to Apollo."

Jimmy already knew that he was to play a major role in the outcome of their conflict, and he was prepared to do whatever it took to save his friends.

"Okay," he said, looking up at Lu Ya and back in Wei Lin's direction. "I'll do my best."

"Your *best* is all we ask, Jimmy," replied Lu Ya. Then, his face displayed concern. "Gorlev's men are coming very soon, but he will not be with them. They will come in the day time, and there will be many. They will be wearing black, and they will have machine guns. Tell your friends."

"It's not the first time, but I'll tell them," Jimmy said, making eye contact with Lu Ya. Lu Ya smiled, nodded to him, and then he and Wei Lin went back inside to rest.

When they had left, Jimmy sat down by the fire, which was still smoking, and thought about his future. He wondered about his destiny, and he contemplated Fate. He wondered if there was any difference between the two and if he had any say in either. Ori had requested his help to defeat Gorlev, and Lu Ya had prophesied that it would all come down to a decision that he had to make, one that would, not only effect his destiny, but the fate of others.

He hoped he would have the strength and confidence when that time had come.

Chapter Two

The Scouting Party

About a month had passed in Chengde, China, and the boys were in desperate need of some recreation. The frost had given way to green vegetation, colorful shrubbery, and bright green ponds. Parelo was turning sixteen in a couple of days, so Jimmy, Ryan, and the others decided to throw him a Chinese birthday party. It was unsafe for them to leave the area, so they made do with what Wei Lin and Lu Ya had on hand for the celebration.

The day of the party, the boys decorated the dwelling, and Wei Lin showed them how to make green eggs, in honor of Parelo and Artemis, and taught them how to cook traditional-style noodles for the celebratory meal.

Ryan, teasing Parelo,

"Sweet sixteen in China, huh, Parelo?" Parelo elbowed Ryan in the side, and then they both laughed. Ryan prepared the eggs, while Jimmy cooked the noodles.

Parelo became serious for a moment, while watching Ryan dye the eggs to represent the Emerald Ring of the Earth.

"I haven't had a birthday since Sazzo was alive," he said, looking down at the brownish-white, bamboo flooring in the kitchen. Ryan put his left arm around his neck.

"Sazzo would have been proud," he said, trying to console him.

"Yeah, man," Jimmy said, overhearing the conversation as he stirred the boiling noodles.

"*Gracias*, *mi amigos*," Parelo replied.

"These noodles keep stickin' together," Jimmy grumbled. Ryan and Parelo chuckled to themselves. "Ryan, come here and see if you can get them apart. They're so long and twisted."

"Yeah, like Wei Lin's hair," Ryan retorted. They all laughed loudly.

Wei Lin came up behind them and cleared her throat. The boys grew silent and turned around to face Wei Lin's agitated gaze.

"Get out my kitchen, before you burn down," she said, glaring at them in turn. "How can learn Kung Fu, but can no cook?" The boys moved swiftly to the door, trying to muffle their laughter.

Later that night, after the celebration, Jimmy awoke to find Lu Ya sitting outside on the steps again. He decided to join him.

"Hello, Mr. Jimmy, have you come to keep me company?" he asked before turning around to see that it was he.

"Yeah," he answered as he sat down adjacent to him.

"Can I assist you with something?" Lu Ya asked, as he sipped his tea. Hesitant, but curious, Jimmy decided to ask him about his gift.

"Why don't you tell us what is going to happen? I mean, you know, don't you?" he asked, looking at Lu Ya. Lu Ya took another sip of his tea before responding.

"My gift has certain limits, you see. I can see glimpses into the future as it relates to myself and those around me. I can't, however, see your end or the end of the world, if that is your meaning. I can only see my end, now," he explained, making eye contact with Jimmy. "I can also see what's about to happen, which is how I knew you were coming outside to sit with me," he said, smiling. "My glimpses are more like visions of the future, rather than premonitions of what will actually happen. They require interpretations, which can become very frustrating."

"I'm sorry, it's just that...everyone tells me that my power has no limitations. That, I can do anything with it. Why can't you?" Jimmy asked, confused.

"Our minds and humanity restrict our abilities, Jimmy. It could be that I don't want to see the end. I don't want to see people hurting or dying. It's hard enough to see my own end," he replied, getting up and moving back into the dwelling.

Jimmy thought about what Lu Ya had told him that night. He realized that he needed to continue to keep an open mind and to stay focused on the mission. The one thing that he didn't want to do was become a hindrance to others or to himself by limiting his potential powers.

A few days later, while everyone was sitting and eating lunch at the table, Lu Ya had a vision. He took a sip of his tea, and then his eyes began glowing. Everyone paused to observe.

"What is it?" Ori asked, concerned. Lu Ya didn't answer immediately.

"They are here...where the Garden used to be," he answered quietly. "We must go meet them."

"How many?" asked Wei Lin.

"Ten," he replied, "dressed in black. They have automatic rifles. We must be careful."

"Is Gorlev with them?" asked Ori, with a determined visage. Jimmy glanced over at him.

"Is the dark man with them?" asked Parelo, apprehensively.

"No," Lu Ya answered. "It is just soldiers."

"Then it's a scouting party. They want to know our location," Ori explained. "Even if we hold them off today, we must leave this place."

They all quickly prepared themselves for a fight, and they made their way outside to confront their enemies.

"Stay close," Ori said to the boys, as he watched Gorlev's men walk up the hill towards the dwelling. "We know what they are after."

"I need to speak to the Ring Bearer of the Silver Ring of Prophecy," the lieutenant in charge stated, as he and his men came to a stop and held their guns at the ready position.

"I am he," answered Lu Ya. "How can I help you?" Wei Lin moved swiftly to his side, ready for any sudden displays of aggression.

"We have orders to take you to Gorlev. You can come peacefully, or we will take you by force. It is your decision," he stated, matter-of-factly.

"I will come peacefully," Lu Ya replied, "But don't harm my friends."

"You have my word," retorted the lieutenant. "No one will be harmed."

Wei Lin looked over at Lu Ya, incredulously, as Ori and the boys stood a few steps behind, confounded by his concession.

"Sergeant, take him," ordered the lieutenant. The sergeant and two other men approached Lu Ya. Lu Ya held out his arms to allow them to cuff him.

Just as the sergeant began to place the restraints on Lu Ya, Wei Lin quickly disarmed the soldier to Lu Ya's right, while Ori threw his staff at the soldier to his left, hitting him squarely in the chest, knocking him down.

Lu Ya grabbed the sergeant's left arm and hit him in the chest with a closed vertical fist, and then he turned him around to face the lieutenant, while holding his right arm behind his back, prepared to break it.

"Not this time," Lu Ya stated, facing the lieutenant. The lieutenant glared back at Lu Ya for a moment.

"Ready!" he began. At this, the men brought their weapons up into firing position. The boys moved up beside Wei Lin and Ori, Jimmy to Wei Lin's left and Parelo and Ryan to Ori's.

They all knew what order was coming next. But, before the lieutenant could give the order, Wei Lin threw her staff like a boomerang, disarming two of soldiers.

"Fire!" the lieutenant commanded.

Ori and Ryan threw their staffs at their counterparts, disarming them, and then they charged forward. Parelo, his eyes glowing, brought forth the Chinese Tiger to attack the two men in the back. They tried to fire on the tiger, but they panicked and ran towards the portal.

Jimmy, eyes glowing, unleashed a wave that struck two of the men, knocking them down. When the men got to their feet, Weil Lin was waiting for them. They pulled out their bayonets and attacked. Wei Lin blocked the one to her right and grabbed the other soldier by his arm. She jumped in the air and kicked both of them in the chest simultaneously, twisting in the air and landing on both feet.

The lieutenant, watching, pulled his pistol from its holster and aimed for Lu Ya. Ori, dispensing with his opponent, turned his attention to the lieutenant.

"Hey, over here!" he shouted to the lieutenant. The lieutenant turned and fired at Ori, but Ori blocked the bullet with his indestructible staff. This gave Ryan enough time to knock the gun out of his hand and to sweep his feet out from under him with his staff.

Lu Ya placed the restraints on the sergeant, and swept his feet out from under him, knocking him to the ground. Then, he ran to aid Ryan.

The lieutenant got up and dusted himself off, as Ryan moved in with his staff in hand. Ryan tried to sweep him again, but the lieutenant jumped in the air, kicking Ryan in the face with his right foot. Ryan's head and body turned to the left, and he fell to the ground, unconscious.

Lu Ya ran up to him, cutting off Ori, as he approached vehemently. Lu Ya stepped up in front of him with a smile.

"Why don't you try that with me," he said, mocking the lieutenant. The lieutenant took a few steps and then wheeled around trying to kick Lu Ya in the head. Lu Ya ducked the spinning kick. The lieutenant tried to hit Lu Ya with a right, but Lu Ya grabbed his fist in mid-strike. He held him by his right wrist, and then he quickly hit the lieutenant in the throat with an open palm in the shape of a snake's mouth. The lieutenant fell to the ground, grasping his throat with both hands, trying to catch his breath.

Near the portal, a man stepped out from behind a tree, from which one soldier had climbed to avoid being torn apart by the Chinese Tiger. Parelo, observing that this man was the Ring Bearer of the Ring of Dominion, quickly used the Tiger Claw to defeat his opponent, and then, as if by means of telepathy, instructed the tiger to attack the dark man wearing the Igbo hat.

The man, not panicking, held out his right arm.

"Sit quietly, kitty," he ordered. The tiger did as he was told. This caused Parelo to stop moving and to slump

29

to his knees, as if in pain. Ori looked in his direction, as the dark man began to head towards Lu Ya.

"Come to me, prophet," he instructed. Lu Ya, with a grimace on his face, had no choice. The Ring Bearer of Dominion had him in his mesmerizing grip. Wei Lin, discarded her enemies with a spinning kick in the air, sending both soldiers rolling down the hill from whence they had come. Then she quickly ran to aid Lu Ya.

"Kneel," the Ring Bearer commanded. Lu Ya, trying to fight, did as he had ordered.

Wei Lin ran up behind him, jumped into the air, and kicked the dark man in the back. The Ring Bearer fell over into the green grass. The dark man turned, glowering at Wei Lin, and then he got to his feet. Ori came over to help Lu Ya to his feet, and the boys ran over to assist Ryan, who was conscious and sitting quietly. The soldiers, along with the lieutenant made their way over to the portal.

"You will die, prophet," he stated, menacingly, "you and all your friends." He smirked at them, and he made his way down the hill as if no one could stop him.

"Get him!" Jimmy shouted.

"No," Lu Ya said, holding Jimmy back. "This is not the time. Soon," he assured him, as they all watched the Ring Bearer open the mystical gate.

"I think you had better explain," Ori admonished, looking curiously over at Lu Ya. Lu Ya simply bowed to him and headed back to the abode.

"Sit down, please, all of you," requested Lu Ya. Wei Lin came over a poured them each a small cup of tea. It was quiet for a few minutes before Lu Ya spoke. Wei Lin gave Ryan an ice pack for his swollen cheek. It was the first time he had actually been hurt, so he was a bit shaken.

"I apologize for my unusual actions. They were not meant to deceive or to harm you all." He took a moment for his words to sink in before continuing. "I knew the Ring Bearer of Dominion was here. I was waiting for him to show himself. You see, he will decide my fate. I have seen him holding me down, and I have seen fire coming towards me. My conclusion is," he paused to glance at Wei Lin, whose eyes were welling up with tears. "That the Ring Bearer will help Gorlev destroy me. I thought that my decision not to follow would change my destiny. I was wrong; the vision remains the same," he explained, half-smiling. "Sometimes, our futures can be altered, but sometimes, they cannot.

"We understand, Lu Ya," Ori replied. "Thank you for sharing, and thank you for your hospitality. I think it may be time for us to leave this place. We will return with more friends and take you and Wei Lin with us. I promise."

The boys tried to hide their excitement because they knew that they were going home. They packed their bags, and then they said goodbye to Lu Ya and Wei Lin.

"In the name of the gods, give us Guardians passage!" Ori stated with authority, and then they went through the ancient portal.

They arrived at the exact time they had left for China. Jimmy quickly moved to the only bedroom in the small home to find Zoonee. He noticed that no one was in the room, but then he heard people talking outside: It was Pazou and Zoonee. Pazou had recovered from the wounds Gorlev had inflicted upon him.

Jimmy turned, opened the front door, and ran outside, jumping off the wooden porch passed the steps.

"Jimmy, your back!" Zoonee said, running to give him a hug. "I missed you," she whispered in his left ear.

"I missed you, too," he whispered back. He looked up and saw Pazou, grinning in the distance. They had been practicing in the field outside Ori's home.

"Pazou! You're okay!" Ryan said, as he jumped over the steps in a dead run right to Pazou's open arms. Parelo ran passed Zoonee and Jimmy at full speed to hug him, too.

"Hello, my young friends! It's so good to see you *back* and *safe*," Pazou said, holding both of them and making eye contact with them.

"Pazou! My friend!" Ori said, as he walked down the wooden steps toward him.

"Hello, it has been a while!" Pazou replied walking over to him. Parelo and Ryan moved swiftly to embrace Zoonee, whom they considered a little sister. Zoonee hugged Ryan and then Parelo, but she noticed the bruise on the right side of Ryan's face.

"What happened? Are you okay?" Zoonee asked, concerned.

33

"Yeah, I just had to save the day, again. You know me: Mr. Hero," he grinned, as the rest of them laughed lightheartedly.

"Well, Mr. Hero, come inside and let me have a look at that," Zoonee retorted, still smiling.

They stayed a little while and visited, and then Ryan and Jimmy left for Ryan's house. On the way out, Ori told them that they would leave in a couple of weeks.

A couple of hours later, Jimmy awoke from a nap to hear his mother and father talking to Ryan's mother over coffee. He sat up quickly and laced up his shoes, and he glanced over at Ryan who was still out. They had to lie to Ryan's mother, Ms. Trigee, about how Ryan had sustained the dark bruise on his right cheek.

"Hey, Jim," his father said, smiling as Jimmy entered the small dining room.

"Hey, Dad," replied Jimmy, as he bent down to hug his mother. Then he made his way over to hug his father. His father winked at his mother as Jimmy hugged him, and she smiled as she sipped her hot coffee. Jimmy and his father had grown closer and more affectionate of late. But neither his father, nor his mother, knew the exact reasons.

34

Only Jimmy knew, and he couldn't divulge the truth as he understood it.

After visiting with Ms. Trigee, they left for home. Jimmy was exhausted, so he entered his room, climbed into his bed, and stared up at his poster of May Sting. As he did, he could only think of Zoonee. His eye lids grew heavy, and he dosed off to sleep for the night.

At school, all Jimmy could think about was Zoonee and about what Ori's next move would be. He thought about what Lu Ya had told him, and he wondered how it would all play out in the end.

"Jimmy?" Mr. Martin asked, "You okay there?" The class chuckled, as Jimmy looked up and nodded at his English teacher. "So, Mr. Rood," his teacher began. "What do you think Emerson meant by the Over-Soul?"

Jimmy couldn't remember his reading. So, he just improvised.

"It has something to do with an alternate reality, where gods are real, and they grant imperfect humans powers to help them maintain the spiritual balance in the universe." His teacher looked at him, curiously, as the rest of the class chuckled at his response.

"Interesting interpretation," he commented. "But, I don't think Emerson would agree with the first part of your exegetical proposal: that gods, plural, exist. But, he might agree that one god exists and empowers us to reach our spiritual potential," he said, nodding, validating Jimmy's thinking and effort.

Jimmy was going to turn fifteen in May, but he was already in the tenth grade, having skipped a grade. Not everyone accepted him, but Mr. Martin appreciated Jimmy's success and natural aptitude for learning. He also liked Jimmy's father, who had purchased new tablets that the teachers could use for presenting their materials.

Jimmy couldn't wait to see Zoonee after school. As he walked over to his table in the cafeteria, a crowd of guys and girls had surrounded Ryan.

"Yeah, I got jumped by three big dudes," he said with a stern look. Jimmy rolled his eyes and sat his tray down across from him. Ryan had a knack for turning potentially embarrassing situations into entertaining show and tells. Jimmy could tell by their smirks that some of the guys were skeptical, but Ryan's farce was a sympathetic hit with the girls.

"Awww, you poor thing," Sandy Rich said, as she patted Ryan's head. *Rich* being the operative word, Jimmy thought to himself. Sandy always had to be in the middle of every dramatic sequence, so she could bask in the attention of her constituents. Jimmy shook his head at the spectacle, while Ryan laid it on thick.

"I picked up a staff and just started swingin' it at bitches," he said, emphatically, coordinating his words with his arm movements. The uproarious laughter caused the vice principal to put down his pizza and to stare over at the boy's table. Jimmy turned around as the vice principal placed his hand on Jimmy's left shoulder.

"A-hem," the vice principal cleared his throat, and everyone quickly scattered from Ryan. Ryan looked up into the eyes of Dr. Wham and quickly began eating his over-salted, extra-cheesy, pepperoni pizza. Dr. Wham squeezed Jimmy's right shoulder, and then he walked back over to eat at the teacher's table.

Jimmy rode home from school with Ryan and his mother, which he normally wasn't allowed to do. But, as far as his mom and dad knew, the two of them still had a science project to complete before school let out for the summer.

"So, how is the science project going, guys?" Ryan's mother asked. Ryan looked behind his seat and grinned at Jimmy.

"Fine Mom," Ryan replied. "It's almost done. Just a couple of more weeks left before it's due."

When they arrived at Ori's, Pazou and Zoonee were sitting outside talking on the porch, while Parelo leaned against one of the cabin rails. They saw Jimmy and Ryan coming toward them and stood up to greet them.

"Hey, you two," Zoonee greeted. "Jimmy, I need your help to catch food for dinner," she said, hugging him around his neck.

Parelo, overhearing her, "Could I help? I think I can help a lot," he said, grinning at both of them.

"Yeah, man," Jimmy replied, "Let's go down to the creek and catch something."

So the three of them went down to the creek that ran through the cave floor and under the road to other side. Jimmy and Ryan had played in the creek multiple times before discovering the hidden cavern. They used to play Wizards and Dragons, swinging from a rope to the other side of the creek, to find the Dragon Master and to foil the plot of the evil sorcerer.

When they arrived, Parelo placed his arm around Jimmy's chest to keep him from going any further.

"Watch this," he said, grinning at Jimmy. He placed his hands out in front of him; his eyes began to glow a bright green, and then several crawfish began to swim towards them. Along with them, catfish and perch began jumping up out of the water. Zoonee positioned herself, eyes glowing, and she froze some of the fish, while Jimmy moved the waters so that the fish would float to the creek bank.

"Awesome!" Ryan said, as he approached them from behind. "You guys are useful. It's too bad you can't fight worth a damn." The others laughed, while Zoonee shoved him.

"At least they didn't get knocked out at the last one," Zoonee said, teasing Ryan.

"Good point! Deep Freeze," he replied, grinning. Jimmy and Parelo laughed as they used their shirts to gather the crawfish. Zoonee created an ice bowl so they could carry the fish back to the cabin.

That night, Jimmy lay in his bed thinking about the day and how much fun he had had with his friends. He had taken down the poster of May Sting, and he replaced it with a mental image of Zoonee that he had seared in his mind forever. Now, when he looked up from his bed, he pictured Zoonee starring back at him, smiling.

Chapter Three

Back to China

It was Saturday, about two weeks later, and Jimmy knew it was time to get back to work. He and Ryan ran to Ori's cabin.

As they approached, they could see Pazou, Parelo, and Zoonee outside training.

Zoonee looked up toward them to greet them:

"Hey, come on guys, can't you run any faster than that," she teased. Ryan and Jimmy looked at each other and then kicked in the rockets, racing each other to the finish line. Once there, they high-fived each other and then went over to the group.

"Hi, Jimmy," Zoonee said, looking into his eyes. She broke eye contact for a second to turn and to look over her left shoulder to see if Pazou was watching. He was; but he simply smiled, as if to understand, and turned to speak to Ori, who had just come out of his cabin onto the wooden, gray porch.

"I...I miss you when you're not around," Zoonee admitted, looking up into his honest, blue eyes.

41

"I...I miss you, too," he confessed, looking down into her shiny, dark pupils. He lifted his hand toward hers, closing his long fingers around her tiny, brown hand. She looked down, and then up again into his eyes and noticed that he wasn't smiling anymore. His gesture was serious, more mature in nature and more intense.

"It's time!" Ori shouted, just loud enough for them to hear and to gain their attention. They both dropped hands simultaneously: They knew that the mission had to be first and foremost in their minds.

They all gathered by the hearth, and then Ori uttered the magic words: "In the name of the gods, give us Guardians passage."

When they arrived, they were all surprised to see that no one came out of the home to greet them.

"Something isn't right, here," Ori stated, as he carefully observed their surroundings. "Be on your guard and spread out. Pazou and I will walk up to the front. You two," he pointed at Jimmy and Ryan, "Go around that side, and you two," he pointed at Parelo and Zoonee, "Go around the other side." They all nodded and quietly, but swiftly, moved into position as Ori had ordered.

"How do we know when to go inside," asked Ryan, anxiously.

"We have to wait for Ori's signal," Jimmy replied. "It could be a trap." Given what they already knew about Gorlev, a trap wasn't simply speculation, but a real possibility. Ryan nodded and remained quiet.

Ori and Pazou knew a Guardian was present; they could sense it. Ori nodded to Pazou, and Pazou reciprocated. Then, Ori opened the sliding door and went inside.

When they were both inside, Ori went one way, and Pazou the other. If it was a trap, they didn't want to be taken at that same time. Ori moved into the room where they all had eaten each day that they had spent with Lu Ya and Wei Lin. He looked into the corner of the room, and there was Wei Lin, unconscious, strapped to a chair.

Ori bent down toward her, carefully lifting her head.

"Wein Lin, Wei Lin," he said softly, until her eyes opened. Wei Lin slowly opened her eyes, but immediately recognized Ori and smiled a rare smile.

43

"Hello, my friend. It is good to see you again," she answered. Ori forced a smile to put her at ease, but was gravely concerned about their predicament.

"It's good to see you, too—friend." About that time, Pazou and the others joined Ori in the room.

Later, Wei Lin explained to them what all had happened, while they all sat at the table drinking tea.

"Gorlev came. He had many soldiers, but Lu Ya and I could have handled them. Gorlev threatened to take my life. When he did, Lu Ya surrendered peacefully. I couldn't believe we weren't going to fight, but Lu Ya insisted. And, so, here I am. I agreed to Lu Ya's wishes," she said, as she sipped her tea, her hands shaking. Ori noticed, and passed her some more bread to eat.

Though Ori and Pazou knew it was Wei Lin's responsibility to protect Lu Ya and the Ring of Prophecy at all costs, he respected her decision. He gently placed his left hand on her right shoulder.

"We will get him back," he stated.

"Yes, we will," she retorted, as she gripped the tiny cup tightly. She looked around the room, and her eyes landed on the two new faces. "Who are these two friendly

44

faces?" she inquired, more out of genuine congeniality then out of suspicion.

"I am Pazou, Guardian of the Diamond Ring of Ice, and this is Zoonee, my Ring Bearer," he stated calmly, bowing respectfully.

"Hi, Asian lady," Zoonee replied, waving her hand and smiling. Wei Lin smiled at her, as if she had seen something in Zoonee's visage that reminded her of herself.

Ori, wasting no time, assumed that Gorlev was now in possession of the Silver Ring of Prophecy, and that Lu Ya might be dead, though he did not speak of it. If this were true, then Gorlev would be able to see them coming. So, a plan, no matter how meticulous, would probably fail. Still, they had to come up with something before moving forward.

The next morning, Ori awoke early, just before daylight, and went outside. As he walked down the steps, he noticed Wein Lin sitting, meditating quietly. He didn't want to disturb her, so he sat down beside her and begin to meditate as well.

After a few moments, Wein Lin opened her eyes and turned her head toward Ori.

"I never had a child," she said, softly, watching the day begin to expand over the horizon. Ori opened his eyes and looked at her, but she kept looking in the direction of the light.

"Lu Ya was my...like my son," she continued. "It is dangerous for us to have children." She turned to Ori, "Did you have a child?"

Ori looking over at her, and for the first time, he noticed a small tear falling from one of her eyes. For the first time, Ori thought, this powerful, wise woman had displayed, what most would consider weakness, but which Ori viewed as bold and beautiful.

Ori slowly moved closer to her and gently wrapped his left arm around her, pulling her into him. He leaned his head in until it came into contact with hers.

"No," he whispered. That was all he said. He didn't share any of his wisdom. He didn't try to explain. He simply sat with her, and they watched the day begin.

Later that day the boys and Zoonee went out to train on their own. It was the first time this had happened. It was the first time that they had been put in charge of their own preparation. This gave them confidence because they felt like they had accomplished a major feat in the stages of their combat training.

Ori, Pazou, and Wein Lin stayed back at the house to come up with a safe plan to rescue Lu Ya.

"Lu Ya will not betray us," said Wei Lin.

"If he is under the power of the Ring of Dominion, he may have no choice," retorted Pazou.

"I'm afraid Pazou is right. We have both seen and felt his power," Ori added, looking back forth at them. "Gorlev will know that we are coming. Somehow, we must plan as if he will know our every move."

"Okay, so, this is what Wein Lin taught us," Jimmy said, demonstrating the Tiger Claw with his powers. As he demonstrated, Zoonee followed Jimmy's movements with her eyes, how the water moved in sync with his arm and hand motions.

After he had finished, he looked at Zoonee.

"Now, you try to do it with me, okay?" Zoonee nodded and got into position. Her eyes began to glow white, and she began learning the style. Ice flowed out of thin air as she imitated Jimmy's movements. Behind them,

Parelo and Ryan stopped practicing and watched as Zoonee seemed to pick up the style with ease.

"She's a natural," Ryan said, grinning in Parelo's direction.

"Yes, she is," replied Parelo, reciprocating Ryan's facial expression.

That night, after dinner, they all met in another room to discuss the plan for rescuing Lu Ya.

"Here is what we know," Ori stated, in a matter-of-fact tone of voice, attempting to make eye contact with each person. "We know that Gorlev will try to get the ring from Lu Ya, or he will try to force Lu Ya to assist him in trapping us. What we don't know is...whether Gorlev will use Lu Ya as bait. Even so, we can safely assume that he knows we are coming, and he may even know when."

After Ori went over the plan to rescue Lu Ya, Jimmy and Zoonee decided to go for a walk. Once they made sure that they weren't being followed, they held hands.

"When this is all over, what are you going to do?" asked Zoonee.

Jimmy thought for a few minutes, and he realized that he wasn't sure. To some degree, he felt that there would always be a mission or a purpose for his powers, whether he was fighting Gorlev or simply helping humanity in some way. Jimmy knew that he wanted to be with Zoonee, and he believed that she felt the same way. He also knew that he wanted to be what he considered normal, but he didn't want to admit this right away. He liked being different. It's what he had always wanted, but he found himself, at times, wanting his life to go back to the way it was before he and Ryan had made their life-changing discovery.

"I'm not sure," he admitted to Zoonee. "I guess I want to finish this first, and then I'll have more time to think about other things."

"Okay," Zoonee said, smiling. "That makes sense."

They continued walking until the day was replaced by the night sky. Jimmy told Zoonee that he wanted to introduce her to his parents the next time he was home, to which Zoonee smiled and said that she would be happy to meet them.

"So, how would you introduce me to them," she asked. Jimmy hesitated, but he knew the response she desired.

"Well, I ..."

Before he could answer Parelo and Ryan jumped out at them.

"Boo!" They said in unison with wide grins.

Zoonee turned quickly and froze them with their hands in the air. Their faces were also frozen solid, and their eyes were as large as golf balls.

Once they were thawed, they all sat around the fire that Pazou had constructed in a hurry, so the boys wouldn't succumb to frostbite.

"You must be careful with your powers, Zoonee," Pazou said, placing his left hand on her right shoulder.

"Yeah, Ms. Freeze First and think later," Ryan said, still shivering under a blanket by the fire on the other side.

"You deserved it! You two scared me!" she said, pointing at both of them. "The next time, I'll freeze something lower!" Ryan and Parelo looked at each other in horror.

"Zoonee! That's enough!" Pazou said, looking at her sharply, as a father. "We are all under a lot of pressure, but we must endure. We must stay focused."

"Pazou is right," Ori said, taking his seat next to Jimmy. We must all come together and work together as one. Otherwise, the plan will fail, and others may be captured or worse."

The boys and Zoonee both nodded.

That night, none of them really slept well, especially Jimmy. He kept thinking about what Lu Ya had revealed to him about his future and about the end of this war. Jimmy closed his eyes to think about what mattered to him and in this way he was able to rest.

"Jimmy! Jimmy!" a voice whispered loudly. It was the voice of Lu Ya. Jimmy woke up in tall grass. The sun was shining as he covered his eyes with his forearm.

"Jimmy! Over here! Quickly now! I don't have much time," Lu Ya said. Jimmy got up and could see that Lu Ya was behind him, up on a hill, looking back at him...waiting.

Jimmy quickly joined him on the hill.

"Lu Ya, are you okay? Where are we?" he asked.

Before Lu Ya could answer, Jimmy realized where they were: He looked up the hill and saw the large white house, and the red barn. He gulped, as he remembered the old cell that held him captive, in which he thought he would die. He felt nauseous.

Lu Ya reached over to him and placed his left hand on his right shoulder.

"It's okay, Jimmy. This is a dream. This is my final attempt to resist Gorlev's torture. Tomorrow, I will give up my ring. Tomorrow, I may be a spirit dwelling with my ancestors. This is why you must listen."

Jimmy turned to catch his gaze. It wasn't one of misery or fear, but one of wisdom and confidence.

"When I make my final move, you must act swiftly," he instructed.

"But, I don't know if I can do it," Jimmy said, questioning his courage.

Lu Ya smiled reassuringly. "Each day that you train, you grow stronger and more powerful. It is the way of the rings. The power that activates the ring is inside you," he pointed to Jimmy as he explained. "It always has been and always will be."

With that, Lu Ya seemed to dissipate slowly, as a cloud.

"Wait Lu Ya! Wait!" Jimmy yelled.

But, he was gone.

Jimmy woke up and it was morning. He could tell by the shadows on the white interior walls. He was sweating bullets, as if he had been running or training for hours. He realized that he knew the *when* but not the *what* of which Lu Ya had spoken. He sat up and could hear voices outside within and without the home. *This is the day*, he thought.

After swallowing his breakfast and barely speaking a word to anyone, Jimmy walked slowly outside and set on the steps. The only one to notice that he wasn't speaking was Zoonee, and she quietly followed behind him.

Zoonee, sitting down beside him,

"So, what's up with you?" she asked, grinning as she lowered her head beneath his eyes.

Jimmy forced a smiled.

"How can you be so cool at a time like this?"

Zoonee sat up straight and stopped smiling. Jimmy wondered if he had insulted her. But Zoonee was simply thinking about how to reply to his question.

"If there is one thing I have learned through all of this, it is to enjoy the small moments and to stay positive," she answered, thoughtfully.

Jimmy looked over at her and caught her eyes fixed on this own. He leaned toward her—

"We are ready, brave ones," Pazou interrupted, with a strong smile.

Red-faced, they both turned to him and got to their feet.

"Let's do this," Jimmy said, confidently.

Zoonee, smiling back at him,

"Yes, Let's."

Chapter Four

The Rescue Attempt

They arrived at the portals and could see the remains of the large white house. They could see no one, but they knew it was a trap, especially Jimmy, who kept his dream and thoughts to himself. He felt that it was better that way: for his friends and for himself.

"De Ja Vu," Ori said, half-grinning. "You would think that Gorlev would choose a different location. His arrogance may give us an edge."

It was morning. Ori thought that it was better to fight in the light. Since it was almost assuredly a trap, he had contended that they would at least be able to see the movements of their enemies...Or, so he thought.

As they approached the bottom of the hill, which gave them some appearance of stealth, Ori went over the plan once more.

"Okay, Pazou and I will go into the house from the basement and attempt to free Lu Ya. Hopefully, Gorlev doesn't have the ring. If he does, this first attempt will not work. When the fighting begins, team two will move to the front to call out Gorlev's men. Team three will move to the rear of the house and go inside. Then, we have to hope for mistakes and hope that Gorlev has not seen the end of this day." He reached out his hand to all of us, and we each placed are hands on top of his and each other's. "Good luck to all. When a team has Lu Ya, signal and we will move with haste to the portals."

We watched as Ori and Pazou snuck up the hill to one side of the red barn. Memories of victory danced in their heads. Like the last the time, the house was unguarded and seemed to be empty. Unlike the last time, they knew it was a trap and that they couldn't underestimate Gorlev.

They watched as Ori and Pazou entered the basement. Minutes later, they could hear sounds of combat.

"We must go, said Wei Lin," looking over at Jimmy and Zoonee. They nodded and hurried up the hill.

Suddenly, fire appeared out of nowhere and surrounded them all. Jimmy's eyes began to glow, along with his ring, and he caused water to appear and directed it toward the flames in front of him. Zoonee joined in, creating a wall of ice around them.

They paused to catch their breaths and to regroup behind the ice wall.

"Did anyone see Gorlev?" Jimmy asked.

"No," Ryan said. Parelo shook his head, along with Wei Lin and Zoonee, respectively. No one had seen Gorlev, but he was there, waiting for them.

As they spoke, the fire began to melt a large hole into the center of the wall of ice. They could see the flames burning through.

"What do we do?" asked Ryan, looking at Wei Lin and then to Jimmy.

"We must fight," answered Wei Lin, and she twirled up onto her staff and over the wall of ice toward the fire.

Without saying anything, Jimmy produced a wave and rode over the remaining flames and wall of melting ice. The others followed.

Once they were over the fire and ice, they began to fight Gorlev's soldiers. Wei Lin twirled her staff, blocking and deflecting bullets. Jimmy generated a large wave and crushed two soldiers. Zoonee, eyes glowing white, froze two others. Ryan twirled his staff to deflect bullets aimed at his chest, and then he rolled to his right and threw his staff at a soldier, disarming him. Further up the hill, Parelo made his way to the house, causing the roots from below to wrap up the soldiers, so they couldn't move. He also summoned crows from overhead to harass and blind the soldiers, causing them to lose sight and focus. He even called on help from all manner of creatures to fight for their cause. The others noticed this display of power and were amazed.

It was clear to all who were present that their abilities had come to fruition, as they pushed Gorlev's army back up the hill. They were winning.

Suddenly, Jimmy saw something that didn't make sense, and he began to feel weak. Zoonee froze Wei Lin while she was in the process of kicking one of Gorlev's men. Ryan knocked Zoonee down with his staff, and Parelo paused fighting and fell to his knees as if he had been hit in the stomach by a battering ram. Then, a few moments later, Gorlev appeared a few yards in front of Jimmy, glowering at him.

"So, you are the key to stopping me?" he said, looking right into Jimmy's eyes. "Well, we will see about that, won't we?"

Jimmy reacted quickly and sent three water balls at Gorlev, but Gorlev sidestepped and the balls of water missed their target. It was apparent to Jimmy that Gorlev had the Ring of Dominion and the Ring of Prophecy. But, Jimmy knew that there were still some limitations and that Gorlev would need more time to master the powers of the rings.

"Well, at least you know whose going to kick your butt!" Jimmy retorted. Gorlev grinned and evil grin.

"Are you sure you are playing for the right team? Join me, and I will release your friends. If you don't, they will all die. You can be sure of that prophecy."

Jimmy looked around and saw that Gorlev's men had his friends. The ice around Wei Lin had begun to melt, but she was still frozen. Zoonee had regained consciousness, but two men had tied her arms. Ryan and Parelo were on their knees, as the Ring of Dominion glowed on Gorlev's finger. Somehow, Gorlev had mastered the powers of the Ring of Dominion, or at least it appeared that way.

Jimmy thought to himself for a few moments. He thought about what Lu Ya had told him. Jimmy knew he could not surrender, but he thought that perhaps this was a necessary step in the right direction, that perhaps his surrender would lead to the moment of which Lu Ya had spoken.

"How do I know that I can trust you?" Jimmy asked. Gorlev turned and walked up to Wei Lin and defrosted her before his very eyes.

"Is this enough proof?" he asked. "Your friends will be released as soon as we have exited through the portal."

Just as Jimmy was about to surrender and go with Gorlev, a staff came flying from out of nowhere and hit one of the guards holding Zoonee, while another staff hit Gorlev in the back, causing him to lose his balance and focus, releasing Jimmy and his friends.

"I bet you didn't see that coming?" Ori said, running down the hill.

Zoonee jumped and flipped over the two guards holding her and froze them before she landed on her feet. Parelo, eyes and mouth glowing green, called forth an eagle and a hawk to chase the two guards that were holding him.

Ryan grabbed his staff and threw it like a boomerang, knocking out four guards.

"Sorry, Frosty, couldn't help myself," he said, smiling at Zoonee.

Jimmy, at full strength and angry, began to glow—everywhere. The surroundings began to vibrate, and everyone paused...

From behind the large white house, giant waves of water appeared. Zoonee, sensing what was about to take place, created a large ice slide from her position to the portal.

"Let's get out of here," she shouted. Ryan, Parelo, and the others quickly joined her. "Jimmy, come on, that's enough!"

Hearing her voice through the sound of the immense waves, Jimmy put down his arms and ran for the slide.

The waves came crashing down on the remains of the white house, the barn, and Gorlev's men. But, Gorlev was already gone. The house was completely destroyed, and Gorlev's men, who foolishly followed him, were swept down the hill, as the water flooded the entire area.

They all looked around at each other and realized that they weren't back home.

"Lu Ya must be here somewhere. I'm just not sure where here is," Ori contemplated, taking in their surroundings.

They were in a wooded area, and they all had a feeling that Gorlev was there, too, hiding or preparing for them. Pazou started a fire, and the rest went out in the woods to search for sticks and for food.

Jimmy walked one way with Zoonee, while Ryan and Parelo went another way.

"What happened back there?" asked Zoonee. "One minute we were winning, and the next...I don't know." She looked up and over at Jimmy, who had grown taller over the past several months.

"I'm not sure," he admitted, "But Gorlev had three rings and knew how to use them. It's taken me almost two years to master mine, and I'm really not sure if I have or not."

Zoonee took Jimmy's hand and they continued walking until they found a small pond where they could catch some fish to eat. Then, they returned to the campfire.

After they had all eaten, Ori began to explain what had happened and where he thought they were for the night.

"I suppose that you are all wondering what happened today. I will try to explain as best I can," he said, looking around at all of them. "I believe Gorlev has killed the Ring Bearer of the Ring of Dominion, which is what he would do to any of you, if you were to give up your ring," he explained, looking specifically at Jimmy. "He has also managed to use the Ring of Dominion to appear invisible to us. He has apparently been training with it."

"That makes so much sense," said Ryan. "Holy crap! How are we going to beat what we can't see?" he asked.

"That's a good question. But, we will figure out a way," replied Ori.

"He also can use the Ring of Prophecy," added Jimmy, though he didn't bother to elaborate. He thought it best not to do so.

Ori suspected that Jimmy knew more, but he didn't say anything in front of the others.

"We were lucky today. Gorlev's men trapped us under some of the rubble from the destruction of the house.

63

It was a trap that we should have foreseen. It took some time for us to get out of the house."

"What about Lu Ya?" asked Wei Lin. "How do you know he is here? You were wrong the last time," she said, looking critically at Ori.

"Yes, I was wrong. Gorlev must be using the Ring of Dominion to influence my thoughts on this matter," he admitted. "I will have to meditate, as we all should, to strengthen our resolve."

"Do you know where we are, my friend?" asked Pazou.

"I believe we are in France. There is an old, abandoned structure to the west. The architecture is French," he assured them. "It may also be where we will find both Lu Ya and Gorlev. In the morning, we will check it out."

The next morning, they woke up and headed for the French building of which Ori had spoken. When they got within several feet of it, they decided to split up again and surround the old, country home. Jimmy and Zoonee went around back with Wei Lin; Pazou went with Ryan and Parelo around to one of the sides to try to enter into a

64

window, while Ori decided to enter from the front. All, except for Pazou, Ryan, and Parelo were to wait for a signal. They all knew, if Gorlev were present, that he would be ready for them.

Ori went inside first and could tell that something wasn't right. The French home was two-stories, so he made his way upstairs. Once upstairs, Ori went into a room to his left. Staff in hand, he looked around the large, rustic room. He saw a chair sitting in the middle of the room with ropes lying on the wooden seat. His first instinct was to call to the others, but he didn't. He was too concerned about their safety, and he knew that they could not afford to lose anymore rings.

Moments later, Pazou, Parelo and Ryan entered the large room. They all saw the chair in the middle, and they saw Ori looking at something on a mantle.

"This is a picture of Gorlev and possibly his mother. Gorlev used to talk about her fondly. She died when he was a boy. He always seemed to blame his father for her death, but he never did explain why," he said, as he took a seat in another wooden chair adjacent to the one which held the rope. "It seems that we are too late. Gorlev is one step ahead of us," he said, looking down at the wooden floor.

Pazou removed the rope from the chair and sat down in it. Then, he looked at Ori and smiled.

"It is not over, my friend. Lu Ya is still alive. There is always a way," he said, determined. "A solution will present itself." Then, Pazou, sensing Ori's dejection, placed his right hand on his left shoulder and held it there until Ori made eye contact with him.

"Well, maybe there is," said Jimmy, who had been standing quietly by the door beside Zoonee and Wei Lin.

That night, they decided to stay in the house. They each took shifts to watch for Gorlev and his men. Before the first shift began, Jimmy sat down an explained what he meant about finding a solution to get ahead of Gorlev.

"One time, Lu Ya spoke with me in my dreams," he said, looking around at everyone in room. "He told me something that I can't share with you guys, but I might be able to see if he will speak to me again and ask him for help. The thing is, is that he hasn't said anything else, and he may not be able to again."

"We respect your decision," Wei Lin said, smiling. "I think there might be a way."

Jimmy looked over to Ori, and he simply smiled, which wasn't the response he thought he would receive.

"Don't know why I didn't think of this before," Wei Lin said, smiling. "Lu Ya has established mystical connection with Jimmy. In ancient times, Chinese medicine used hypnosis, which was created by Zhou, God of Dreams. I will try to hypnotize you and call on Zhou to aid us while you are under."

Jimmy looked up at Ori in horror.

"It will be okay, Jimmy," he said calmly, reassuringly.

"Make him think he's Zeus," said Ryan, "Then he can shove a lightning bolt straight up his..."

"Okay, Ryan," Ori interjected, "We get the picture, son."

"My bad," Ryan grinned.

Wei Lin proceeded to give Jimmy instructions. Jimmy looked up at Zoonee, and she smiled down at him as he lay on an old, tattered brown sofa. Everyone was watching and offering their support to Jimmy.

"Good luck, *Amigo*," Parelo said, smiling.

"May the Gods be with you Jimmy," Pazou said, trying to boost his confidence.

"Okay, Jimmy, watch my medallion and try relax," she said in a soothing tone.

Jimmy nodded and watched the medallion oscillate back and forth. As he watched, he wondered about the origin of the medallion.

Chapter Five

The Road to Zhou

Once Jimmy was under, Wei Lin continued to give him instructions and to ask him questions.

"Jimmy, I invoked Zhou, God of Dreams to aid us. You may see him and be able to speak to him. You on his turf, now. He will guide or deny you. Be prepared to defend you cause and yourself. He's ornery god," at that Zoonee and the others smiled, but did not speak, to avoid interfering with the process. "Do you understand, Jimmy?"

"Yes," he answered, his eyes closed and arms by his side.

In the hypnotic state, Jimmy found himself on a dirt road somewhere in China. He followed the road. He didn't have any sense of time, and there was nowhere else for him to travel. On the way, he passed three different people from different walks of life. He passed a Chinese aristocrat, or so he thought.

"Hi, can you tell me where I can find Zhou? I really need his help?" he asked. The aristocrat, dressed in a dark Tang suit, looked at him from top to bottom, circling him. He wasn't really walking, Jimmy observed; but rather, he was gliding around Jimmy, taking him all in.

"What is your name, peasant?" he asked in a condescending manner. Jimmy turned his head to try to meet his eyes. "Don't look me in the eyes at this proximity before introducing yourself!" he shouted and glared at Jimmy. "Do you have no respect?"

Jimmy, a bit unsettled, decided to play along.

"Forgive me," he said, turning and kneeling before him. "I am not familiar with your ways. I mean no disrespect. My name is Jimmy Rood, and I am from Newford, Arkansas."

The aristocrat's face softened, but he didn't act pleased about it.

"Very well, Jimmy Rood," he said, and then disappeared into smoke.

"Are you okay, Jimmy," asked Wei Lin, looking a little concerned.

"Yes, I'm okay," he replied.

"Where are you?" she asked.

"I'm walking down a dirt road, somewhere in China, I think," he answered.

"Remember, Jimmy, Zhou is a god. It may not be easy," she explained.

Jimmy continued walking down the dirt road until an older man wearing a conical paddy hat, associated with a farmer, crossed over to his side and began walking or gliding toward him. When he was within a few feet of Jimmy, he paused and looked up at him.

"Help me, please. My family hasn't eaten more than a little rice and bread for months," he asked, holding out his dirty hands to Jimmy and then kneeling.

"I-I don't actually have any money, sir. I don't know if I can help you. I would like to. I just don't have any money," Jimmy answered, kindly.

The old beggar looked into Jimmy's eyes for a few moments, and then he looked down at his right hand, which held the Azure Ring of Water.

"Kind Sir, what about your beautiful ring? It would feed my family for months. We would be forever grateful," he said.

"I-I don't think I can. I need it, you see, to defeat an enemy. I would if I could," he explained.

The old beggar looked up into Jimmy's eyes once more. Then, he looked down.

"Very well," he said, and turned to leave.

"Wait! Please!" Jimmy shouted. "Here, for you and your family."

The old beggar turned back, and Jimmy took off his ring and placed it in the old beggar's dirty hand. The beggar looked at it, turned to Jimmy, and then smiled. Then, the old beggar turned and walked away with the Azure Ring of Water.

"They're gonna kill me," Jimmy said to himself and continued walking.

"Why are we going to kill you, Jimmy?" asked Wei Lin."

"You can hear, me?" asked Jimmy.

"Yes, Jimmy, we can hear you," answered Wei Lin.

"Oh, cool," he said, nervously.

"Concentrate Jimmy," instructed Wei Lin. "I don't know how long this will last."

"One question: Can you hear everyone else?"

"No, only you," she replied.

"Okay, good. I'm safe for now."

Jimmy continued on, hoping that he would soon meet the God of Dreams and be able to help, not only his friends, but Lu Ya as well.

Finally, Jimmy came to what appeared to be a portal to some place. It was located in mid-air and surrounded by white pillars on both sides. As Jimmy contemplated going through the portal, a Chinese woman wearing Hanfu clothing and carrying a golden staff appeared and glided over to him.

"So, Jimmy, is it?" she asked. "You are our hero, right?"

"I don't know, ma'am, but my name is Jimmy, Jimmy Rood," he answered.

"You don't know." She walked over to the portal, and she moved her arm and hand in a whisking motion, and then Jimmy could see his friends waiting in the country house, watching, wondering what was taking place. "See your friends?" she asked, rhetorically. "They are all watching and waiting on their hero. But, you, Jimmy, are not sure. You have doubts, and so you put them in danger."

Jimmy didn't know how to respond. He looked down; he looked at his hand, which held no ring, no power. The woman, with jet-black hair, small black eyes and a creamy white face, gazed at him.

"No, you are not the hero of the gods, are you?" she mocked. "You gave up your ring. You are just a boy," she jeered. "Let me show you what happens to little boys who try to wield the power of the gods." She moved swiftly behind him, and whisked her hand, showing him a different scene.

Jimmy could see himself over Ori's dead body. He could see Pazou, his face sweaty, and Zoonee, crying and shaking with no ring on her hand. He saw Ryan and Parelo, faces dirty, hands burned by fire. Parelo had no ring.

"This is what our Guardians have sent to us. You, a boy, who will fail! How can you defeat Gorlev?" she mocked.

Jimmy's heart beat until he thought it was going to burst out of his chest, and he began to perspire as he could feel the heat from the scene and sense the emotions. He began to cry.

"Yes, you are just a boy. Why did you come here? Why do you offend us?"

Jimmy spoke. "Stop please. Stop showing me this!" he said, angrily.

The woman looked at Jimmy with scorn.

"Make me."

Jimmy turned to face her. The woman's eyes grew large with surprise and anticipation. Jimmy remembered the Tiger Claw and he displayed the form he had learned and prepared to battle the apparition. She chuckled to herself, and then she thrust her staff at him. Jimmy caught it and then brought his hand around to her face, but she disappeared and reappeared behind, sweeping his legs out from under him. Jimmy twirled in the air, but landed on one knee and glared sharply at the woman.

The woman chuckled at him, again, but then Jimmy stood up, closed his eyes and brought his hands together as if to pray.

"Poseidon, Father of the Azure Ring of Water, hear me, please," he pleaded.

Suddenly, the Azure Ring of Water appeared on his hand. His entire body began to glow a bright blue, and he opened his eyes and looked straight into the eyes of the woman.

Jimmy, eyes glowing blue,

"Lady, I don't know who you are—but this is not what you want," he warned.

The lady smiled, placed her staff by her side, and spoke.

"Very well, walk through portal, hero."

Jimmy, body still glowing, walked through the portal.

Once he was on the other side of the portal, Jimmy stopped glowing and became weak, so he sat down on a rock to rest. He thought it was odd that he could feel tired in a dream, but then he knew dreams were like that sometimes.

He looked around, observing his surroundings. He saw a small hut on the other side of a stream and began to walk toward it. After he crossed the stream, he saw a short, round figure come out of the hut.

"Hello, Mr. Jimmy, I am Nun Ta, a representative of Zhou, God of Dreams. He sent me to meet with you when you passed all three tests.

"Tests? What do you mean? Those were just tests?" Jimmy asked, confused.

"Yes, Mr. Jimmy, they were just tests—but necessary," he said looking at Jimmy with his small, dark eyes. Nun Ta sat down on a large stone and began to draw something in the dirt. Jimmy observed that Nun Ta was an older, Chinese man with a dark goatee and long dark hair. Nun Ta drew the first figure, then the second, and then the third.

"The first apparition you met was a wealthy landowner. He examined your pride. To have too much, brings failure. But, too little, brings oppression," he explained. "You passed!" He pointed to the next figure.

"To be a true hero, you must be willing to sacrifice yourself for the cause of others. You passed!" He said, grinning up at Jimmy.

"Finally," he said, pointing at the third figure. "You must have faith, if you expect to challenge and beat Gorlev, Mr. Jimmy. You passed! This is why you were granted an audience with Zhou. Understand?"

"Yes," Jimmy answered.

"Now, to the reason that you came so far today," he smiled, wiping the dirt off his hands. "Sit down beside me, please, and be very quiet." After a few moments, what looked like another, smaller portal opened and Jimmy could see Lu Ya, sitting in a chair, weak, with his hands and feet tied. He looked as if he had been tortured.

"Lu Ya, Lu Ya, hear Zhou, God of Dreams, commands an audience," he said with authority.

Slowly, Lu Ya's head began to rise. Lu Ya knew couldn't speak with his mouth, so he spoke with his mind.

"Jimmy, I knew you would find a way to me," he said. "Gorlev is coming for you and your friends. He plans to burn the house down with you all inside it and keep you there, surrounded until you all burn. Then, he will relieve you of your rings," he explained.

"Can he hear me?" asked Jimmy.

"Yes, speak to him, now," answered Nun Ta.

"Where are you?" asked Jimmy.

"I am not sure. They placed me in this room, and then they took off my blindfold. I think I am in Germany in a home. I heard some music playing earlier; it sounded like it might be German."

"I know where you are, and we are coming. Just hang on!"

"I will Jimmy. Thank you."

With that, Nun Ta ended the connection. Jimmy knew what he had to do next, but he still had some questions.

"Does Gorlev know that I was able to communicate with Lu Ya?" he asked.

"No, Gorlev can't see in this realm, Mr. Jimmy," he said, grinning. "But, if you and your friends are not able to defeat him in your realm, then ours will not be safe for long," explained.

"Remember, Mr. Jimmy, the essence and power of the gods is contained in the *Seven*. It is what we refer to as the rings. The gods can help you through them and through faith."

"Will we beat Gorlev?" asked Jimmy, making eye contact with Nun Ta.

"How should I know, I am just a messenger," he shrugged, but when he looked up at Jimmy his eyes where larger, darker. "Good luck, Jimmy," he said, as his voice boomed.

"Zhou," he gasped.

"You okay, Jimmy," asked Wei Lin, as she peered down at Jimmy. Jimmy's vision was blurry, but his eyes quickly adjusted. He sat upright, and gulped.

"I know where Lu Ya is!"

Chapter Six

The German House

When Jimmy was brought out of the hypnotic state, he began to explain what all he had seen and heard. The others listened, intently, to all that he had to say.

"So, what do you need us to do, Jimmy?" asked Ori.

"We need to get out of here, now," he instructed. But, it was too late. Gorlev and his men were coming down the road and firing their weapons at the old house.

Bang! Bang! Bang! is all they could here for several seconds. They all lay flat on the floor as pictures, small particles of rock, and stuffing from the couch began to flow through the air.

"We have to get upstairs," instructed Ori. "Be careful, but hurry!"

They all listened and began to crawl to the staircase. Once they were in front of it they were able to run up without fear of being hit by a bullet. Once upstairs in the large room, they barricaded the door and stayed away from the only two windows in the room. Then, Jimmy remembered what he had failed to mention.

"Oh, god! He's going to burn it down—with us inside," he said, frantically. "I'm sorry, I forgot to tell you. We have to get out of here."

"Okay," Ori said, picking up a chair and throwing through the larger window. "Jump!" he ordered.

"Better, still," said Zoonee, as she created an ice slide to the ground from the second story window. One by one, they all slid down. Ori was the last one. He checked the door; and, as Jimmy had said, smoke was coming into the room from underneath the door.

As soon as Jimmy landed, he bolted for the front. He wanted to fight Gorlev, and he was tired of running.

"Jimmy wait!" said Ori, but it was too late, Jimmy had already rounded one side of the home. "Wei Lin, get them to the portal. Pazou and I will stay and get Jimmy." Wei Lin, nodded and took Zoonee, Parelo, and Ryan and went down through the woods.

After running several yards, Zoonee stopped, turned and ran back to the house. The others didn't notice that she was gone until they had started back up the other side and began to head toward the portal.

"Where the *hell* is Zoonee?" Ryan asked. Wei Lin and Parelo turned toward Ryan. "Oh, sorry, excuse my language."

"She must have gone back to help," said Parelo, looking at Wei Lin for instructions.

"I will go back," she said. "You two clear a path to the portal. We will save the others and Lu Ya."

Jimmy engaged with two soldiers, deflecting bullets and knocking them down with large bursts of water. His sights were on Gorlev, who was near the back, behind a line of four German soldiers. Gorlev saw Jimmy and grinned a sinister grin. Then, he held out one of his hands and motioned for Jimmy to come to him, taunting him.

Ori and Pazou came around the other side and used their staffs to deflect bullets. Then, they used them to jump over a group of three soldiers, while the soldiers, leaning back, tried to fire straight up at them, missing. As soon as Ori and Pazou landed they threw their staffs at the feet of the soldiers, knocking them down and causing them to drop their weapons. Ori and Pazou quickly used their staffs to destroy their weapons.

Jimmy quickly disarmed the four soldiers with large bursts of coiled water that appeared right in front of them, swallowing them up. One of the bullets managed to graze Jimmy's leg, but he didn't feel it right away. He was focused, his eyes, mouth, and body glowing bright blue.

Ori and Pazou, realizing that they had not been able to deflect all the bullets, held their wounds and watched, as Gorlev and Jimmy sized each other up for battle.

"Leave him alone," Zoonee ordered, her body and eyes glowing a bright white. She came over and stood to fight alongside Jimmy. The two of them began the Tiger Claw form, as Gorlev stood, grinning.

Gorlev's eyes began to glow purple, which was a signal to Jimmy and Zoonee that he was about to use the power of the Amethyst Ring of Dominion. Before he could get ready, Jimmy rammed him with a swirling wave right to the gut, which knocked him back into a large tree and to the ground. Zoonee, seizing the opportunity, froze him where he stood. But, in seconds, Gorlev melted the ice and ran through the woods.

"After him!" Jimmy shouted.

"No, we must leave now, if we are going to save Lu Ya," said Ori. "We will get him, Jimmy, just not today."

Jimmy and the others moved quickly to the portals. When they arrived, they noticed that Ryan and Parelo were dusting themselves off and that Wei Lin wasn't with them.

"What happened?" asked Ori, looking concerned.

"Wei Lin and I stopped Gorlev from going through," answered Parelo. "She went after him. They went that way," he said, pointing into the woods off the road.

"Pazou and I will go after her. The rest of you go save Lu Ya," he instructed. Jimmy didn't like the plan, but listened and led the way through the portal.

When they arrived in Germany, they were angry and focused. The two guards by the door were no match for Jimmy, as he thrust them backwards with waves into a wall, breaking two large pictures. Two others came out, and Ryan hit one in the chest with his staff, while Parelo kicked the weapon out of the hands of the other one. Then, he head butted the guard, pulled him down and flipped him over into a small end table where a lamp stood.

Jimmy went down the hallway in search of Lu Ya. One guard came out of a room, but Jimmy bent down and rolled toward him, dodging the bullets. When he came up, a wave of water came up with him and suspended the guard against the ceiling, while Jimmy's eyes grew an angry blue. Zoonee came down the hall and froze the soldier, and then Jimmy dropped him.

Jimmy created a wave to smash in the door where Lu Ya was being held, and he disarmed the two guards in the room. Zoonee came in and froze both of them. Jimmy moved to the middle of the room and untied Lu Ya.

"We have to go back. No time to explain," Jimmy said. Lu Ya looked up, exhausted, hungry, thirsty and weak.

"Not you, Jimmy," said Lu Ya. "You must stay. Gorlev will know that you are coming, just like he knows you are here." Jimmy paused and stood up, looking in Ryan and Parelo's general direction.

"We will go," Parelo said. Jimmy nodded, and Ryan and Parelo headed back down the hall to the portal.

Jimmy and Zoonee stayed with Lu Ya and moved him to a bed in another room, so he could rest better. As soon as Lu Ya's head touched the pillow case, he was fast asleep.

Jimmy, whispering to Zoonee,

"Let's go in another room and let him rest." Zoonee nodded.

"Why didn't he want you to go?" Zoonee asked. "Doesn't Gorlev know where we all are?"

"I'm not real sure. But, when I can I'll ask Lu Ya."

They sat on an old auburn sofa and spoke softly to each other. Zoonee took Jimmy's hand.

"We almost had him, huh?" she asked, smiling up at him.

"Yeah, we did," Jimmy answered, smiling back at her. "I hope they can handle him without us."

"Me, too," said Zoonee. Then, she eased over and lay her head in his lap and fell asleep. Jimmy looked down at her and ran his fingers through her fine, black hair. *I don't know what I would do without her*, he thought to himself. Then, he too, fell asleep.

When he awoke, Zoonee was standing over by a window looking outside. It was dark in the room, except for one lit lamp. Jimmy looked over at the table by the lamp. The book that he and Ori had found, over a year ago, was still there. He got up and moved over by Zoonee.

"Look at that lady," she said. "She looks as if she is waiting for a bus or something. She has no idea what could happen to her or her world if Gorlev wins." She turned to Jimmy. "What did Zhou tell you?"

Jimmy thought for a minute before answering. He knew he couldn't tell her about one of the scenes that involved Ori's death and her crying.

"I had to pass three tests before I could talk to him. I passed them, which I think means that I have what it takes to help us defeat Gorlev," he explained. "That's all I really know. He showed me a few things from the future," he admitted, looking down into her dark eyes. "But, I don't know if I'm meant to share them." She nodded.

"I understand," she said, as she placed her arms around his waist to hug him.

"We need to check on Lu Ya," Jimmy said. "I need to ask him some questions."

Jimmy and Zoonee went back into the room with Lu Ya, who was awake, but staring up at the ceiling. He heard them come into the room.

"It's strange to not be able to see anything coming," he said, "To only be able to use my senses and logic to interpret future events," he said, sitting up in the bed. "How are you both?"

"I think you know the answer to that," Jimmy said, half-smiling.

"Can't be all bad, Jimmy. You are here with friends. Though, it is very hard to be what we are," he admitted, smiling again.

"How do you feel, Mr. Ya," asked Zoonee.

"Better, now that you two are here."

Jimmy couldn't wait any longer to question Lu Ya.

"Why didn't you want me go?" asked Jimmy, intently.

"Because Gorlev is tracking your footsteps, Jimmy, not the others," answered Lu Ya.

"So, if he is only tracking me, then he knows I'm here, but doesn't know where my friends are, right?" he asked.

"Very good, Jimmy, that's right. It takes time to master the power of rings. You know that. Gorlev would not be ready to see the footsteps of everyone. But, the longer he has the ring, the sooner he will be."

Jimmy had one more question for Lu Ya.

"I have one last question. But, you don't have to answer it," he said, looking down at the floor and then up at Lu Ya.

"It's okay, Jimmy."

"Why were you captured if you could see Gorlev coming?"

"Because I saw it all play out," he answered, "from several different perspectives. If they had taken Wei Lin, she would have been tortured and killed. It was my best option. Now, our futures may end differently," said Lu Ya. Jimmy nodded. He remembered the scene with Ori and how painful it was, so he understood why Lu Ya could not give up his Guardian.

"Anything to eat?" he asked. "Anyone else hungry?" They all smiled and went to find something to eat and to drink.

After they finished eating and drinking what they could find, they began to think about the others, wondering if they were safe or not.

"Do you think the others are okay," Zoonee asked, concerned.

"Fighting Gorlev, alone, is challenging, but he is even harder to defeat when he uses machine guns," said Lu Ya.

"It's only him," replied Jimmy.

"Oh, good. Then, they should return safely."

That night, Jimmy didn't sleep much. He was on first watch and was supposed to rotate with Zoonee who was asleep on the sofa. Jimmy didn't know if he could wake her or not. He didn't want to disturb her, and he felt that Lu Ya needed a good night's rest.

As he sat in a rocking chair in the corner of the living room, he began to think about Lu Ya's prophecy concerning himself, what the female apparition had shown him, and he also began to question Ori's decision-making.

We had him! We could have ended this war! What was Ori thinking! He began to wonder if, when the time had come, Ori would allow Gorlev to be destroyed. *Would he be able to destroy his childhood friend?*

As Jimmy thought about this question and others, he drifted off to sleep.

Chapter Seven

Back to Newford

The next day Jimmy woke up to the sound of many voices. The others had made it back, and they were all celebrating their small victory. They had saved Lu Ya, and found Wei Lin. Though they had sustained minor injuries, they were all safe and back together again. Ori and the others felt it was time to go home to rest.

"Hey, Bro, we get to go home," Ryan said, half-hugging Jimmy. Parelo came over and listened in on the conversation.

"What happened to Gorlev?" asked Jimmy. The others wanted to forget about Gorlev for a while, but they humored Jimmy.

"Well, Wei Lin was kickin' his butt, when we found her. But, then, he did the whole disappearing thing and vanished through the woods," answered Ryan. Ori came over and elaborated.

"Gorlev has been well-trained with the Amethyst Ring of Dominion. He has most likely killed his ally, the Ring Bearer. He can force us to see what he wants, now, which is very dangerous for us. Some of us are wounded, and we have rescued Lu Ya. This is a good time to go home and regroup." He placed his good arm on Jimmy's shoulder and smiled.

Wei Lin was speaking with Lu Ya, and then she saw Jimmy, who walked slowly down the hallway and entered the room where they had held Lu Ya. He was wrestling with wanting to go home, but also wanting to attack Gorlev while he was vulnerable, while his minions were few. He now believed that Gorlev could be defeated, if everyone attacked at once. Wei Lin knocked softly on the wooden door.

"Come in," said Jimmy, who was hoping it was Ori and that he had reconsidered going home.

"Hi, Jimmy," Wei Lin said as she slowly moved toward him. She reached out for him and hugged him. "Thank you, Jimmy, you saved my Ring Bearer." Jimmy half-smiled and nodded, but Wei Lin could tell something was bothering him.

"What is wrong, Jimmy?" she asked, taking one of Jimmy's hands, with a concerned look on her face.

"It's just that we had him, didn't we? The first time? Ryan even said you had him. Shouldn't we attack, now?" he asked, intensely.

"I know how you feel. We all do. I want kick Gorlev's head off," she said, which caused Jimmy to smile a little.

"Then why don't we. You and I could do it," he suggested. "No one else has to get involved. No one else has to get hurt or captured." Wei Lin, still holding one of his hands, placed her other hand on his right cheek.

"You hero, Jimmy," she said. "Truly, you are hero. Everyone here. Everyone is okay...because of you. But, you mustn't be driven by anger or impulse. You must be patient, Jimmy. Allow mind to rest. Enjoy time with friends and family. Remember: They are reason we here, okay?" Jimmy nodded and knew she was right.

They went back down the hall together. When Lu Ya saw them, he motioned to Jimmy to come over to him.

"Again, thank you, Jimmy," he said, placing his left arm around him. Zoonee came over after patching up Pazou and took his right hand, looking up at him. She no longer cared that everyone knew that she had feelings for Jimmy.

After they had finished celebrating, they all decided that it was better for all of them to be together. So, they gathered at the portal, and Ori said the words.

Once back in Newford, Jimmy and Zoonee walked away from the others, so they could speak privately.

"I'll miss you, Jimmy," she said, looking into his eyes. She placed her arms around his waist and hugged him tightly.

"I'll miss you, too," he said, holding her close.

"Hey, come on. Let's go," hollered Ryan. Jimmy looked up and grinned, but Zoonee sharpened her eyes and glared at him.

"Oh, my bad. See ya Miss Ice," he said and he and Parelo quickly ran to the cave.

"I better go," said Jimmy, moving some pieces of hair away from her eyes.

"Okay, Jimmy. I'll see you in a few days," she said, hugging him one more time.

As he was leaving, everyone came outside to see him off. He turned to see everyone waving, and so he waved back. Then, he entered the cave with Ryan and Parelo who were waiting.

When they got back to Ryan's house, Ryan hugged his mother like he hadn't seen her in days, and introduced Parelo.

"Hey, Mom, this is Parelo Jenkins," he said, enthusiastically. "He lives in a house behind the old cave. You actually have to go through the cave to get there. Cool, huh, Mom?"

"Yeah, I guess," she said, a little suspicious. "Nice to meet you Parelo." She held out her hand to shake Parelo's. Parelo grinned as he shook her hand.

"Nice to meet you, too, ma'am," he responded. Ms. Trigee noticed he had an accent.

"Where are you from, Parelo?" she asked, curious.

"Brazil, ma'am," he answered.

"Mom, stop the interrogation. He's cool. Can he stay the night, please?"

"Sure, he can, if it is alright with his mom and dad," she said, looking back at Parelo, smiling.

"It's cool, Mom, we asked already," said Ryan. "Come on, Bro, let's go to my room."

"Well, okay, but shouldn't I at least call his parents?" she asked, calling after them.

But the boys were already in Ryan's room. While Ryan and Parelo played video games, watch movies and ate popcorn, Jimmy listened to music using Ryan's iPod8. He wanted to relax and to keep his mind off the future.

The next morning, the boys and Jimmy's dad all gathered at the table for breakfast. Jimmy's dad drank a cup of coffee and spoke to Ms. Trigee, while the boys ate pancakes.

"Watch this," said Ryan, as he threw one of his pancakes up in the air and caught it with his fork as it was about to hit the table.

"I'm really impressed," said Parelo, grinning.

Jimmy chuckled a little to himself. He was glad to be back home and to see that Ryan was still Ryan. He observed that the other-worldly circumstances had not changed his friend. He wished that he could say the same for himself.

It was Sunday, so Jimmy and his father worked on some laptops out in the garage.

"School year is almost over, huh?" asked his father.

"Are you ready for the eleventh grade?"

"I guess so," answered Jimmy. "I don't think it will feel much different until my last year."

"That makes sense," said his father. "Hey, pass me the thermal paste, please."

It was usually small talk with Dad, Jimmy thought to himself. But, Jimmy knew it was important to him.

As was their new routine, Jimmy and his Dad watched a game together after working in the garage. That night, Jimmy lay in bed thinking about Zoonee, wishing he could see her every day. He felt that he was torn between two worlds, and he had to be a different person in each one.

"Good morning," said his mom. His mom was a morning person, but his dad wasn't really. Jimmy thought it was a little odd, too. His mom smiled at him over a cup of coffee. "You two about finished with the science project?"

"Yeah, Mom," he said, reaching for a bowl for his cereal. His mom had made French toast, but Jimmy didn't really care for it, though his dad liked it. "It should be finished in a few more days"—*a few more days in another realm*, he thought to himself.

Jimmy observed his mom making out the bulletin using her smartphone. She squinted through her glasses. She could borrow a school tablet for this task anytime, but new technology tended to make her nervous. *She stuck with what she was used to*, Jimmy thought to himself.

At school, during lunch, Ryan was entertaining his fan club with his tall tales and new exploits. *It was a good thing that they didn't take him seriously*, thought Jimmy.

"Yeah, Parelo—that's my buddy from Brazil—and I took on these two soldiers. One had a machine gun and the other one had a pistol. I blocked the bullets with my indestructible staff, while Parelo used his telekinetic power to make tree roots come out of the ground and wrap up that mother huncher," he said, as the group of listening students laughed.

In his English class, Jimmy tried to stay awake while Mr. Martin interpreted lines from *Romeo and Juliet*, which is how they were going to finish out the year. Jimmy couldn't really identify with the storyline, as it was, but it did make him think of Zoonee. When Mr. Martin spoke of Romeo's love of Juliet, he would think of Zoonee, and it would give him butterflies.

On the ride home, Jimmy thought about the butterflies, and he thought about love. He had never been in love before, so he didn't really understand it. He compared Romeo's feelings for Juliet to his feelings for Zoonee. *Would he do anything to see her? Yes,* he thought. *Would he do anything to protect her? Yes,* he thought, again. *Would he die for her? Yes.* Jimmy now knew that he was in love with Zoonee. But, he didn't know what to do about it.

The next day at school, Jimmy decided to talk to Ryan about it. He was pretty sure Ryan had never been in love, nor had he ever had a girlfriend, but most of the girls liked him and thought he was sweet and funny.

"So, what do you think about *Romeo and Juliet*?" Jimmy asked. Ryan looked up from his cheesy, triangular piece of pizza and peered into Jimmy's soul.

"Finally, you see it, don't you?" he grinned. "We all see it, man."

"See what?" Jimmy asked, trying to play it cool.

"For the *love* of the gods," he said. "You are in love with Zoonee, Bro."

"Well, how do you know?" Jimmy asked.

"Please, man, all you do is daydream about Ms. Ice," he said, smiling and taking another bite of his pizza.

"Well, okay, let's say you're right? I'm in love. What do I do next? Do I tell her?" he asked.

"Yeah, you could. But, if I were you, I would write a poem for her. Yeah, you could call it Ice Water," he suggested, grinning.

"Keep it up, and I will tell Zoonee," Jimmy threatened, glaring at Ryan.

"Okay, okay, take it easy. I feel you, Bro. But, really, a poem might be a good place to start."

Later, Jimmy lay on his bed watching a game while trying to write a poem for Zoonee. He wasn't having much success, so he sent a text to Ryan asking for help.

To: Ryan

From: Jimmy

Jimmy: I need help w/ poem. I'm stuck.

Ryan: tell her she has a nice ice lmao

Jimmy: You are lucky she doesnt have a phone—lmao

Ryan: lol okay think about her features and the way she makes you feel

Jimmy: she looks good and makes me feel good

Ryan: this is gonna take some time

That night, Jimmy and Ryan worked on a rough draft of a love poem for Zoonee. Jimmy planned to type it up in Keyboarding II the next day, and then he was going to have Ryan deliver it when he went to Ori's to get Parelo for the weekend.

A couple of days later, the poem was ready, and Jimmy gave it to Ryan.

"Don't forget to give it to her," Jimmy said.

"I got you, man," said Ryan, "Don't worry."

It was Friday afternoon and Jimmy was nervously awaiting a text from Ryan. He was also hoping that Ryan hadn't forgot. Jimmy had written and revised it several times before giving it to him to give to Zoonee.

He went over it again:

Your dark eyes capture me;

I cannot look away;

Your face hypnotizes me;

I cannot look away;

Your dark hair wraps me;

I cannot move away;

Your beauty freezes me;

I cannot move away;

The butterflies empower me;

They will never fly away.

It was 5:00 pm, so Jimmy decided to text Ryan.

To: Ryan

From: Jimmy

Jimmy: Did you give it her?

Ryan: no man, I forgot

Jimmy: what?

Ryan: just kidding lol yeah she liked it. She can't wait to see you.

Jimmy: Thanks, man.

This news made Jimmy feel very happy and excited.

"Jimmy, can you come in her, please?" called his mother.

"Yeah, Mom, I'm coming." Jimmy went into the dining room with a large smile on his face. But, when he looked at his mom, she didn't look very happy and neither did his dad. Jimmy gulped.

"Sit down, Jimmy," said his dad. Jimmy was checking his memory for any misdeeds or misconduct, trying to infer the reason for this ominous meeting. He looked at his mom who looked at him sharply and then back down at her coffee. Then, after a few long minutes, his mom spoke.

"I spoke with Mr. K, today," she paused, "And can you guess what he told when I asked about your science project?" His mom glared at him and so did his dad, who seemed as uncomfortable as Jimmy did. *Busted*, Jimmy thought to himself. "Don't worry, Ryan's mother knows, too," she added. "Tell me the truth, and I might shorten the number of days that you are grounded." Jimmy thought to himself: *I can't tell them the truth. If I do, they will have me institutionalized.*

"It's a girl. There is a man that lives behind the cave. His name is Pazou, and he has a niece named Zoonee. She's about my age, maybe a year younger. Me and Ryan made it up, so we could go over there. She has a brother named Parelo. Parelo spent the night with us last weekend. If you don't believe me, you can ask Ms. Trigee.

His mom looked over at his dad, as if to get his opinion on the matter.

"It sounds reasonable," he said, shrugging. "I probably would have lied, too." His mom sharpened her eyes at him, but then she softened them when she looked back at Jimmy.

"Okay, but you are still grounded for lying to us. Two weeks," she said, holding up two fingers. Jimmy nodded, and then got up from the table and walked to his room. When he did get grounded, two weeks was the standard, though it was never explained why. He couldn't go anywhere, so he couldn't see Zoonee until the end of the school year and the beginning of summer. He still had his phone, so he sent text messages to Ryan to find out what his punishment was and to see if he could go see Zoonee for him to deliver messages.

To: Ryan

From: Jimmy

Jimmy: They found out about our science project. I'm grounded for two weeks. Nice plan.

Ryan: yeah, me, too. this what we get for trying to save the world, huh? but, we can't tell them, man. they'll put us away or send us to a shrink.

Jimmy: I know. hey, can you sneak out to tell Ori and Zoonee.

Ryan: yeah, man, no problem. I'll go tonite.

Jimmy: Tell them I'm sorry. I'll be there when I can.

Ryan: i'm pretty sure it will be okay.

Jimmy: Okay, see ya later.

Ryan: Okay, man.

It was Sunday, and Jimmy was helping his dad finish repairs on some computers. There was an awkward silence until his dad went over to a cooler and grabbed a soda for each of them.

"Here," his dad said, tossing him a soda. Jimmy caught it with ease, which surprised his dad a little. He observed that Jimmy had grown taller and looked stronger, though Jimmy never worked out. "You been working out at Ryan's?"

Jimmy knew it was hard to keep secrets from his parents, and it was even harder to get away with lying.

"Sort of," he said, feeling that this was the best answer. His dad nodded, accepting his vague answer, and they both went back to work.

The next day, Jimmy had just gotten to his locker and opened it when Ryan walked quickly to speak with him. He grabbed Jimmy's arm to get his attention.

"Hey, you need to come with me," he said, in a serious tone. Jimmy gave him a confused look but followed him to the boy's bathroom.

"What's wrong?!" asked Jimmy. "Is Zoonee okay?!

"Shhhhhh! Quiet, man, remember where we are," said Ryan. "Yeah, Zoonee is okay; everyone is okay. But, Lu Ya and Wei Lin, along with the others went back to China to their home to get somethings, some valuable things. But, when they got there, it was burnt to a crisp, Jimmy—to a crisp. They lost everything. Ori is furious and believes Gorlev is hunting us. He thinks that, if we don't go after him, he could come to Newford."

Jimmy's worst fears were beginning to come true. If Gorlev couldn't get the rings, he was going to hurt us in other ways, by attacking our homes and family and by keeping us running from place to place. *He had to be stopped. If not stopped, prevented from coming to Newford*, Jimmy thought to himself.

"He can't get to Newford, man," he said, heading for the school entrance, "no matter what the cost. If Ori won't take action, then we have to," Jimmy said, resolutely, holding a fist in the air. Ryan just nodded, a little concerned by Jimmy's demeanor. When no one was around, the two of them bolted and headed to Jimmy's house, which wasn't more than a mile from the school.

Once they arrived, they had to figure out a way to get to Ori's cabin.

"Now what?" asked Ryan, panting and placing his hands on his knees, trying to catch his breath. Jimmy looked around for his dad's old pickup truck. He got in. The keys were in the ignition, so Jimmy started it up.

"Get in," he told Ryan, as he rolled down the window.

"We are gonna be in so much trouble," replied Ryan. Then, he got in the truck and they headed to Ori's home. On the way there, Ryan had questions for Jimmy.

"How are we gonna get away this?"

"Easy, we will arrive at the same time we left. We will bring the truck back, and then get back to school before it ends. We should only miss first period," he explained. "We just need a reason. I'll say I was feelin' sick or something, and you were in the bathroom watching out for me."

"Solid plan, Bro. I'm proud of you," he said, grinning. "Just don't kill us, okay?" Jimmy had his permit, and he would be sixteen in about a year, so he wasn't too concerned. He had also driven to Ryan's with his dad on a few occasions. He knew, though, that Ryan was right to be concerned if anything did go wrong. The penalty would be more than two weeks. He knew he was in danger of losing his parent's trust during a pivotal time and also losing access to his friends, especially Zoonee.

Chapter Eight

The Payback

When they arrived at Ori's cabin, Zoonee ran down to greet Jimmy with a big hug. They both squeezed each other tightly for several seconds.

"Get a room," Ryan said, laughing. Zoonee glared at him and flipped him the bird.

Everyone came outside and Ori began walking toward Jimmy. Jimmy and Zoonee broke apart to hear what Ori was going to say.

"Hello, Jimmy. I assume that Ryan has shared the latest new with you."

"Yeah, I'm ready when you are," Jimmy replied.

"Good," Ori smiled, placing his right hand on Jimmy's right shoulder. "Come inside, and let's formulate a plan."

After they had gone over the plan, they all gathered in front of the hearth. They were all ready—and they were all angry.

"In the name of the gods, give us Guardians passage!"

They arrived at the portal in France at the location of the French, country home. They knew it was a trap, but no one cared. They all felt that it was their turn to strike back. Jimmy and Zoonee were out in front; they lead the way. Ori and Pazou covered one side, and Wei Lin, Ryan, and Parelo covered the other.

"Show yourself, Gorlev. We are ready for you," said Jimmy. Just like that, Gorlev and his men appeared on top of the French home. Gorlev threw fireball after fireball down at them. His men took aim and fired. Other men appeared and began firing at them from the ground. There were more men than ever. Gorlev, too, was prepared.

As soon as Gorlev appeared, Jimmy created a large wave and sent it crashing into the home, rocking it and causing some of Gorlev's men to lose their balance and fall off the roof of the country home. Zoonee quickly froze several of the men on the ground, while Parelo caused many of the trees around them to fall to shield them from the bullets and to crash into the home. Gorlev and his men were forced to exit the roof.

Wei Lin and Ryan disarmed and fought several men on the ground, deflecting bullets and twirling up above them and then landing behind them, sweeping their legs out

113

from under them or knocking them unconscious. Parelo summoned black birds, which darkened the skies and attacked the men on the ground, so they couldn't fire.

Once Jimmy was sure that everything was going according to plan, he took off after Gorlev. He needed to face him, one on one. Four men fired at Jimmy, but Jimmy used the Tiger Claw form and deflected the bullets and created a wave at the same time that slammed into them, knocking them out and relocating them.

Gorlev, seeing Jimmy, used the Amethyst Ring of Dominion to appear invisible to Jimmy. Jimmy could feel the effects, making him a little weak. But, his entire body was still glowing a bright blue, and he looked around for any sign of Gorlev. Gorlev threw three balls of fire at him from out of nowhere, but Jimmy easily shielded himself from them with a thick plate of water.

Jimmy searched for Gorlev behind the home, but he couldn't find him. The weakness had left him, so he inferred that Gorlev must have gone back to join the battle in front. He quickly created a huge wave and used it to carry himself up onto what remained of the country home. He looked down to see the others fighting and winning. His friends had dispensed with the majority of Gorlev's soldiers. Zoonee had frozen many of them; and, seeing Jimmy, decided to join him on top of the home. So, she created a slide, and began to run up it to Jimmy.

But, suddenly, she screamed, and disappeared. Jimmy could feel the weakness again.

"No! Zoonee!" yelled Jimmy. "Come out and fight, coward! Let her go!"

Gorlev did let her go. Still appearing to be invisible, he threw her off the roof of the home.

"No!" Jimmy yelled, and created a large body of water under Zoonee to slow her fall and to move her to a softer place to land. But, as he did, Gorlev appeared behind him and hit him in the back with a fireball, setting his clothes on fire. Jimmy rolled to put out the fire. But, as he did, Gorlev created a blow torch of fire and sprayed it down from the roof of the house at his friends. Ori and the others were forced to retreat as Gorlev's fire consumed his own men, the trees, and anything else that stood in its path. Zoonee was unconscious in the grass, and there was no one but Jimmy to stand against him.

With everything below on fire, including the home, Gorlev turned his attention back to Jimmy. He let Jimmy get to his feet.

"So, Water Boy, you refuse to join me," he said, gazing at Jimmy, his arms crossed. "You see, you can't defeat me. I have seen it." Jimmy tried to throw two balls of water at him, but Gorlev knew they were coming, moved and hit Jimmy in the chest with a fireball, setting fire to the front of his shirt. Jimmy cringed in pain as he turned over on his chest to put the fire out. He had sustained multiple burns, but managed to get to his feet. Gorlev was toying with him.

"One more chance, Jimmy," he said, eyes glowing, body glowing a bright red. Gorlev gathered his strength and created a fireball large enough to consume his entire body. "Give me your ring, or die," he said in a menacing voice.

Jimmy looked down, he couldn't see his friends because of the flames. He could feel the roof of the home about to give way beneath him. He could hear the cracking below. He met Gorlev's gaze with one of his own.

"Never! I will never give you the ring!"

"Very well," Gorlev replied.

Then, Jimmy remembered the tests. He remembered what each apparition had told him. He passed them all. He was a hero. Gorlev threw the ball of fire at him, but Jimmy's skin became water and the fire couldn't burn him. He began to walk toward Gorlev, who was astonished and frightened by what he witnessed.

"Another time," he said, and became invisible and was gone.

The roof caved in, and Jimmy with it.

When Jimmy came to, he was in a bed in Ori's cabin. He was sore, but he was alright otherwise. Zoonee noticed and immediately hugged him and kissed him on his right cheek.

"Are you okay?" she asked, standing beside him and holding his hand. Jimmy sat up.

"Yeah, I'm just a little sore," he replied. He noticed that he didn't have a shirt on and that his injuries had healed. "What happened?"

"I saved you before you hit the floor of the house. But...," she paused, "there was something else," she said, making eye contact with him.

"What? What did you see?" Jimmy asked, anxiously.

"Water." Just then, Ori stepped in the room.

"Sorry, I don't mean to intrude, but I need to speak with Jimmy, please," he said. Zoonee hugged Jimmy once more, and then she left the room. "How are you, Jimmy," he asked, looking concerned. Jimmy got up out of the bed and stretched.

"I'm a little sore, but I'm good. I feel fine," he replied.

"Good. Do you have questions about what happened?"

"Yeah, a couple," Jimmy smiled. Ori smiled back.

"It seems that you have tapped into more power from Poseidon's ring. When Zoonee went in to save you, your molecules had turned to water. Consequently, they saved you from the fire. What happened to Gorlev?"

"When I changed, he ran," Jimmy answered. Ori looked away for a moment. He seemed to be thinking.

"Do you know why you changed, Jimmy?" Jimmy shook his head, but then he remembered the tests and what the apparitions told him.

"I...I think it had something to do with the tests I passed when Wei Lin hypnotized me," he answered.

Ori nodding,

"Fascinating. I have never seen anything like that before, Jimmy," he admitted. "You have mastered your power." He got up and came over to him. "I'm truly proud to be your Guardian," he said, and then he turned to leave.

"Ori--," said Jimmy, "I didn't do anything to cause the change." Ori looked at Jimmy, his eyes grew larger.

"The power of the ring protected you. You and the essence of the ring are one, now," he smiled. "If there is anything that you can share with the others, then please do so. It could save their lives, too, and it could mean certain defeat for Gorlev."

Jimmy nodded as Ori left the room. He sat back down on the edge of the bed to think about what Ori had told him. Then, he realized that he had to get back home.

He ran outside, and went up to Ryan.

"Hey, man, you okay," he asked.

"We, gotta get back," Jimmy said.

"Oh, yeah, I forgot!" Replied Ryan. They quickly said bye to the others and took off to the cave.

Once they were back at Jimmy's house, it was 8:35. They were going to miss first period. They ran as fast as they could, snuck in the side door of the school by the band room, and headed to the boy's bathroom at the end of the hall by the library.

As soon as the bell rang, they went to the office to tell Jimmy's mom that he got sick before first period and had to go the bathroom. Ryan stayed to watch out for him. Fortunately for them, Jimmy's mom believed them. They had pulled it off.

They didn't have time to really explain why they had to leave in such a hurry, so Jimmy had Ryan sneak out and do it later that night. He sent a text to him to make sure

Zoonee wasn't mad at him and to make sure they all understood.

To: Ryan

From: Jimmy

Jimmy: So, how did it go?

Ryan: its cool man. they know and understand. Zoonee sends her love lol.

Jimmy: Good. I was worried.

Ryan: later Water Man lol.

Jimmy: lol later

That night Jimmy thought about what had happened and what Ori had told him. He wondered if it was something that was just going to happen, or if he would be able to control it, or call upon it when he needed it. He also thought about what Lu Ya had told him. *When would that happen? Would it still happen since we saved him?* There were still questions that he needed to be answered before the inevitable, final conflict that he saw during the tests.

Then, he switched and thought about Zoonee. He thought about how worried he was when she was thrown off the roof of the country home. He wondered if they had made the right decision by going after Gorlev. They were all safe, but Gorlev had escaped. They had won the small battle, but Gorlev was still alive. For the first time in his life, Jimmy knew that Gorlev had to die, but he wasn't sure that he could do it. He wasn't sure that he could take a life.

Chapter Nine

The Unanswered Questions

Two weeks had gone by, so Jimmy's parents gave him permission to stay the night at Ryan's again. His dad was driving him there, and Jimmy could hardly wait to see everyone, especially Zoonee. Usually, his father didn't say much, but Jimmy could tell that there was something on his mind.

"Son, I know that you don't feel comfortable telling us certain things, but always know that we are here for you, okay?" Jimmy nodded and gave his dad a half-smile.

When they arrived at Ryan's, Jimmy placed one leg out of their car and reached down to grab his bag of clothes.

"Oh, Son, when you get back, I'd like to know how my pickup held up the other day." Jimmy gulped and looked up at his dad. His dad simply smiled.

As soon as Jimmy and Ryan got to the cabin, Zoonee ran up to Jimmy and hugged him—and then she kicked him.

"Owww!" Jimmy looked at her, confounded.

"You can't run off like that! I don't care if you get into trouble! You had me worried!" she said, her eyes glowing white. Ryan, who was listening, fell to the ground as if he had been hit in the head by a large object, laughing and rolling on the ground.

"I-I'm sorry. I didn't think," he said, bending over and holding his left shin. When Zoonee heard his apology, her eyes quit glowing and she lunged at him, hugging him harder than before.

Parelo walked up and smiled.

"Hey, Jimmy, Lu Ya wants to see you," he said, so they all followed him back to the cabin.

Lu Ya was sitting on Ori's old, tattered gray sofa beside Wei Lin. He looked up and smiled.

"It's good to see you, Jimmy," he said. "I heard about your transformation: Incredible. We were all just talking about it." Lu Ya didn't come with them to the last battle. Ori and others felt that he needed to rest, so he stayed at the cabin.

After visiting and eating dinner with everyone, Zoonee motioned for Jimmy to come outside with her. Parelo and Ryan were waiting, and they all walked down to the creek where they had caught fish to eat. Jimmy could tell that something was on their minds, as they didn't speak much on the way there. Zoonee looked up at Jimmy.

"We want to know what happened. How did you change?" she asked in a serious tone of voice.

"Yes, how did you do it?" asked Parelo. "I didn't even know it was possible."

"We all want to know, man. That was some seriously bizarre stuff...and you know how bizarre I am," said Ryan. They all chuckled a little, but then they became serious again. Jimmy sat back on a large rock, looking downward and then up at them.

"The truth is, I don't know. There was so much happening all at once," he explained. "I mean, I thought I was going die." No one spoke or made a joke. They were all listening. "I remember being afraid, afraid of losing you," he said, glancing into Zoonee's eyes. "I also remembered that I couldn't give Gorlev the ring, no matter what. Then, I remembered something from the time Wei Lin put me under, something about passing the tests."

"What tests, Jimmy," asked Zoonee, puzzled. *Should I tell them? How much should I tell them?* Jimmy thought to himself.

"When I was under, I met three different people. They each tested me to see if I was ready to meet Zhou."

"You met Zhou, huh?" asked Parelo, who took a seat next to Ryan.

"Yes," Jimmy said.

"Why didn't you tell us?" asked Zoonee. Jimmy had an answer, but he didn't want to share it. He couldn't share what he saw with them.

"We are all in this together, *Amigo*," said Parelo.

"You don't have to do this alone, man," said Ryan.

"I know...I just..."

"You can't do this alone," interrupted Parelo. "You can't." Jimmy knew he was right.

"Okay, then we have to train. We have all have to figure this out—together," replied Jimmy.

"Okay, Jimmy, show us how," Zoonee said.

Jimmy and the others went out into the field by Ori's cabin to train. They started with what Wei Lin had taught them and then they began dueling to practice their combat skills. Parelo and the others observed that Jimmy had not transformed.

"Why haven't you changed?" asked Parelo.

"I'm not sure. Maybe it has to be a life or death situation," Jimmy answered.

"Keep trying," said Zoonee. "This is important for all of us." Jimmy nodded. Parelo and Jimmy dueled. Parelo sent several rocks flying at Jimmy, but he just created waves with his hands and deflected them. A small one managed to slip through and hit him on the shoulder. Jimmy rubbed his shoulder, as the others looked on, failing to understand why he couldn't change for them. They believed that, if he couldn't change, then they couldn't change.

Ryan and Jimmy gave it a try. Ryan threw his staff at Jimmy, but Jimmy just created a wave and flipped over it, as the staff sailed below him. *Nothing*, Jimmy thought. Next, Zoonee was up. Zoonee fired an ice ball the size of a bowling ball a Jimmy, but he simply created a wave to deflect it, and it went flying into the woods to his right.

Jimmy paused for a few moments, scratching his head.

"Maybe it's not about control. Ori said that the essence of the ring and I are one," he explained. "Perhaps it only reveals itself when I really need it. I mean, we are just practicing. But, if it were real, then maybe..."

"But, what about us," said Parelo. "There must be something else."

"Parelo's right," said Ryan. Zoonee nodded.

"Let's take a break, and then try again, later," she suggested.

Later that day, Jimmy went to speak to Lu Ya about the tests and what the apparitions revealed to him.

"Hey, can I talk to you privately for a minute?" asked Jimmy.

"Of course, Jimmy," replied Lu Ya. Then, he got up off the sofa and headed outside with Jimmy.

"What's on your mind, Jimmy?" asked Lu Ya, patting Jimmy on the back as they both stood on Ori's wooden deck.

"How do you know if our future is still the same?" asked Jimmy.

"I don't know about your future, Jimmy," he paused. "Well, not anymore. I do know what my end will be, and I am proud to accept my fate."

"So, what you told me about it"—

"It will not change, Jimmy," Lu Ya reassured him, patting him on the shoulder.

"How do you prepare, knowing your end," asked Jimmy.

"No one really wants to know, but I felt that I had no choice. We are all key players in this war, Jimmy. Each of us must understand his or her role. My role is that I must sacrifice my ring and my life for the good of many," he elaborated.

Jimmy accepted his answer and explanation, but he didn't like it. He didn't like the idea that a person's fate could not be changed. He went back inside. Everyone was sitting around the room talking, laughing, and enjoying each other's company. Zoonee looked up at Jimmy, and he could feel the butterflies. He decided to focus on them for the time being.